POLO'S
PONIES

POLO'S PONIES

A NICK POLO MYSTERY

Jerry Kennealy

St. Martin's Press
New York

Library of Congress Cataloging-in-Publication Data

Kennealy, Jerry.
   Polo's ponies / Jerry Kennealy.
      p.   cm.
   ISBN 0-312-02267-0
   I. Title.
PS3561.E4246P64   1988
813'.54—dc 19   88-11587
                                                                         CIP

First Edition

10   9   8   7   6   5   4   3   2   1

For my brother, Don, and
my sister, Patricia

POLO'S
PONIES

1

"He's a bookie," I said.

"Bullshit," Jane Tobin replied, in that special voice of hers. She uttered the word with all the authority of Arnold Palmer yelling "fore" as a stray golf ball heads for the gallery, and with all the sincerity of Ollie North reciting the Pledge of Allegiance. It was something she had picked up as a sportswriter for the local morning paper. She was one of the first women writers to enter that last bastion of male supremacy, the locker room. The fact that she was so attractive—auburn hair, creamy skin with just a small band of freckles visible across her nose, and enormous green eyes—made the job tougher for her. She had to put up with a lot of guff at first, but she eventually won the respect of most of the players because she was so good at what she did. Now she was a three-time-a-week columnist for the same paper, writing on everything from politics to the weather. Whatever struck her fancy. And today her fancy was horses. Specifically racehorses. Jane could discuss rebounding with Larry Bird, baseball strategy with Billy Martin, and zone defenses with Joe Montana, but when it came to horseracing, she was a complete novice. Which was one of the reasons I was her date.

"What would a bookie be doing at a racetrack?" she asked.

"There are people at the track who like to bet at high limits, and they'd rather take odds that are a little lower from a bookie than have to pay income tax on their winnings. But his main job is to be a stopper."

The object of our discussion, Johnny Aiello, was standing about twenty yards away from us, scanning the jockeys and trainers with a pair of powerful binoculars. A short, heavyset man in his late sixties, he was wearing his usual track outfit: an oversized raincoat and battered felt hat.

We were standing alongside the paddock at Golden Gate Fields racetrack, located just north of Berkeley and across the bay from San Francisco. The paddock, in case you're not familiar with the sport of kings, is where the horses are put on display just before the race. They're brought out by the grooms and paraded around in a circle, then blankets and saddles are put on, and the horses are trotted around again, so the would-be sharpies can check them over to see if they're moving well, or if they look overanxious, too sweaty, or not sweaty enough. There are a dozen things to look for before plunking down their bets. That's the would-be sharpies I'm talking about. The real pros, like Johnny, don't pay nearly as much attention to the horses as they do to the jockeys and trainers.

"And just what the hell does *stopper* mean?" Jane asked.

"Off the record?"

She made a clucking sound with her tongue and shook her head. "Yes, off the record."

"Say a horse is listed in the morning line at twenty to one. That's the official opening bet. The real odds are determined by the amount of money bet on the horse at the track. A bettor can place a bet with a bookie anytime from a few days before the race until just minutes before post time. If the bookie suddenly finds himself overloaded with bets on one race, at high odds, he'll wonder if the heavy bettors have inside information and he'll try and protect himself by having someone at the track bet enough money to drive the odds down. Or he can start a bandwagon." Jane looked at me skeptically. "Now, if the bookie gets a lot of early action on that horse going off at twenty to one, he'll want to drive down the odds right away, so he has his man make a big bet just after the betting windows open. This may drive down the odds to three to one. The bettors at the track figure this must be smart money, inside stuff, so they jump on the band-wagon, driving the odds down even further. The horse may end up going off at even money, all because of that big first bet. Now take this particular bookie, notice anything unusual about him?"

"Ummm, not really, except he has a cane."

"It's a beautiful day, the temperature is around seventy-five, but he's wearing a raincoat. Remember the old Marx brothers movies? Harpo had this coat that held everything from a toaster to a rubber duck. This bookie's coat is lined with extra pockets, but there're no rubber ducks in there, just cash."

"But how does he know when or if to make such a

bet? You told me that there aren't any public phones at the track."

She was right. If you wanted to use a phone you had to go to the security office, and they would tape and monitor your call. "In the old days they had runners, young guys that would be stationed at the nearest pay phone to the track. They'd literally run in relays, like in the Olympics, only instead of passing the baton, they passed on the latest order from the head man. Now, with all the new electronic gear, it's a lot simpler."

The horses were through parading. The jockeys got their final instructions from the trainers, mounted up, and were led out onto the track.

"Five minutes to post time," I said. "We'd better get our bets down."

We had to walk right by Johnny. He caught my eye and gave a small nod. At one time, when I was a kid, we had been pretty good friends. He even played Santa Claus for me once. But my joining the police department had put a crimp in our friendship. Even after I'd left the force, and then gone to prison, he had kept his distance. We would nod and exchange hellos, now, but that was about it.

"Hi, Johnny. How's everything with Uncle Pee Wee?"

"Hello, Nicholas." He always managed to pronounce my name so it came out *nickel-ass*. "Sometimes good, sometimes not so good."

I introduced him to Jane, and he doffed his stained fedora. "My pleasure, *bella donna*."

"Who do you like in this race?" I asked.

He ran his thumb and index finger down his face, as if to wipe the wrinkles from his cheeks. "Stay away from

4

number seven. He doesn't want to run today. I like the four horse, and so does his trainer." He looked briefly at his watch, nodded to Jane, and shuffled away.

"My good wishes to Uncle Pee Wee," I said to his retreating back.

"What an interesting man," Jane said. "Why does he whisper like that?"

"The only time a Sicilian whispers is when he has a knife between his teeth. Johnny talks like that because he had his Adam's apple smashed in a fight a long time ago."

"He said the seven horse doesn't want to run today. Is the race fixed?"

"Fixing a race is harder than you think, not that it hasn't happened. But sometimes a trainer doesn't want his horse run very hard, maybe's he's coming off an injury, or maybe he figures the horse just can't win this race and he wants to save him for the next one. That's why Johnny was using the binoculars. He can read lips."

Jane gave me another of her "bullshits."

"And just who the hell is Uncle Pee Wee?"

"He's really my uncle, and he's the bookie Johnny works for."

2

We walked from the paddock to the grandstands, then to the escalator. It takes two escalator rides to get from the grandstand to the Turf Club at Golden Gate Fields, and you have to stop at each level and be inspected by shoving your hand under a special light that shows up the purple stamp you had pressed on when you bought your entrance ticket. It always reminded me of the times in high school when you left the dance to sneak out to the car and have a couple of beers, and they wouldn't let you back in if you didn't have your hand stamped. Of course at the track you didn't have the school principal sniffing your breath as you went by.

The grandstand is where the regulars bet. General admission. It only costs a few bucks to get in. The floor is cement, there are several bars, and you can buy pizza, nachos, chili, and hot dogs. The next level up is the Club House. Here the customers dress a little better, you walk on linoleum, the booze costs a little more, and the food is sandwiches with hand-carved meats.

The Turf Club is air-conditioned, the floor carpeted in emerald green, and the seating at little tables with fresh white linen and flowers. In front of the table is a color TV, which gives the odds on the upcoming race and then telecasts the actual race once it starts. Polished brass handrails separate the tables. The booze is expensive, and lunch is a buffet of salads, roast beef, turkey, halibut, and an array of desserts including cheesecake and fresh croissants.

I've always been a grandstand man myself, but Jane had free passes, and who was I to turn my back on the power of the press?

There are seventeen pari-mutuel windows, and on the weekends, they're all operating, but since this was midweek, only nine were open, and they weren't doing much business.

I put ten to win on the number four horse Johnny had recommended. Jane bet five to win on number six, because it had such a cute name, Poco Paco.

I placed the bets, then met Jane back at our table in the super-exclusive Directors Room. She was chatting away with a middle-aged man with an eighteen-hole tan and hair the color of silver. Old, expensive silver. He kept smiling, then letting his eyes bounce down to the cleavage made apparent by Jane's scoop-necked blouse. I didn't blame him. It was an impressive sight, all the more so because it was rather recent. Jane had been married for six years to a stockbroker. She caught him fooling around with more than just the Dow Jones average, and divorced him. Jane's mother was so happy about the divorce the first thing she did was buy Jane what she called a good boob job. "Let that bastard drool when he sees you now," she said. The silver-haired dude was doing a little drooling as I edged in and handed Jane her bet ticket.

Introductions were made and we all had a drink and watched the race. The four horse came in at three to one.

Jane pouted briefly. "I should have listened to your friend Johnny."

"Always go with the pros."

We ordered another drink, and the discussion turned to horses. Mr. Silver Hair owned several Thoroughbreds, and Jane had been raised on a farm in Stockton and knew something about the care and feeding of horses, so they got along famously. Personally I don't like anything about ponies, except that they pay off for coming in win, place, or show.

We handicapped the next race. Jane, sticking to her cute-name theory, went for the longshot.

I stopped at the men's room before making the bets. There were the usual three urinals, one so close to the ground it must have been put there specially for jockeys. The floor and walls were black and brown terrazzo. I was alone, doing what I had come to do, when I heard a soft, buzzing sound.

There were two stalls at the end of the room. The tip of a wooden cane stuck out from under the door.

"Are you okay in there?" I asked.

No answer. I peeked through the stall's slightly opened door. Johnny Aiello sat perched on the toilet, his head back and bent sharply to the right, his eyes opened wide, a bunched-up handkerchief stuck in his mouth.

Checking for his pulse seemed a stupid thing to do, but I did it anyway.

In his right hand he held the handle of his cane, attached to which was a slim, wicked-looking six-inch blade. There was blood on the blade. He looked as if he were about to fall off the toilet seat, and I tried to position his body so that he wouldn't drop to the floor. He was fully clothed, his pants still up and belted. I opened his raincoat and patted the inside pockets. They seemed full. The buzzing sound was coming from a small plastic box clipped to his belt. It was a pocket pager, the type where computerized messages are printed across a small screen in green letters. The message kept repeating: r5, #6, 5g.

I unclipped the pager and dropped it in my pocket. I was in a daze as I wandered back into the Turf Club. A deep-voiced announcer boomed out the message that there were only two minutes to post time. I scanned the tote board. It was the fifth race. The number six horse, Trish's Lamb Chop, was listed at twenty-two to one. I dug out my wallet and money clip and ended up with a two hundred and sixty dollar bet on number six.

I had a drink at the bar and watched the TV set as the horses broke from the gate. Trish's Lamb Chop took the early lead. She never relinquished it, going from wire to wire, a full four lengths ahead of the three glistening thoroughbreds thundering behind her, fighting for second place. The final odds were 19.10 to 1, meaning that for every two dollars bet, a winning ticket paid forty dollars and twenty cents.

For a man who had just won over five thousand dollars I didn't feel so good. The first thing Jane asked me when I got back to her table was, "Are you feeling all right?" The second thing she said was, "Your zipper's open."

3

Not only am I lucky enough to live in San Francisco, I live in what is the best neighborhood in the town, North Beach. When I was a kid the Beach was almost a hundred percent Italian. Now it gets eroded every day because of the unbelievable real estate prices. In another ten years or so, it'll be just another place bursting with yuppie condos. I knew the end was in sight when the fast-food franchises got a foothold in among the mamma-poppa restaurants, shoe repair businesses, and grocery stores. It seems every time one of those places goes under, the next morning there's a new bank or savings and loan in its place.

We had a saying when I was a kid growing up in the Beach. "Valente Marinied." As in, "Did you hear Paulie's father Valente Marinied? Got hit by a truck." Or, "Poor Mrs. Donitello Valente Marinied last night." Nobody ever out and out died, they all "Valente Marinied." The basis for this unusual cultural habit was the Valente Marini Funeral Parlor, which was located right in the heart of North

Beach, on Green Street. Italians from all over town came to this particular funeral parlor for the "final-final." The place had changed hands, and was now simply called the Green Street Mortuary, but the old-timers still ended up there.

Johnny Aiello was no exception.

The mortuary was jammed, people spilling out into the hallways and onto the streets. There were so many flowers in the room where Johnny was laid out, it was hard to breathe. I paid my last respects, and made my way over to where my uncle was standing.

My uncle and I were about the same height, a shade over six feet. He got the nickname "Pee Wee" because his brother, my father, stood some six feet three. He was dressed all in black: suit, shoes, and tie. The immaculate white shirt made his handsome face stand out.

"Nicky, good of you to come," he said.

I took his hand and pulled him closer, then reached into my suit pocket and passed him the pocket pager I'd taken from Johnny Aiello. "We have to talk."

He nodded his head. "The Café. As soon as this is through."

That was an hour and a half later. Italians take their funerals seriously. I saw dozens of people I knew and hadn't seen in years. My one and only tenant, Mrs. Damonte, was there too, which shouldn't have been a surprise. A day without a wake is like a day without sunshine to Mrs. D., a five foot tall, eightyish bundle of energy who paid me about the same amount of rent she had paid my mother and father when she moved into the bottom unit of the flats I lived in. I raised the rent on her once, and once was enough. She acted as if the flats were hers; and she took over possession of the garden and most of

11

the basement, gracefully allowing me enough space to get my car in. She had her good points: The garden was filled with fresh vegetables and spices and she kept the place clean. In fact my main concern was that the cement in front of the property was going to be worn down to nothing thanks to her constant sweeping and hosing.

She gave me what from her was a smile, the lips breaking slightly upward a quarter of an inch, then put her funeral face back on.

After the rosary I drifted outside. An unmarked police car was double-parked across the street. I walked down the street to Capp's Corner and had a glass of red wine. The place started to fill up with people from the funeral parlor and I gave up my stool to a man I knew only as Guido. He was in his seventies and still operated his own little fishing boat out of Fisherman's Wharf. His hands were thick with calluses and cuts and he almost squeezed mine to pieces as we agreed that it was a shame that poor old Johnny Aiello had Valente Marinied.

Uncle Pee Wee's office is located in The Café, a small bar and espresso shop on Columbus Avenue, just a couple of blocks from the mortuary. I had been in there dozens of times and had never seen anyone sitting at the bar. The tables were always packed with tough-looking old men dressed in cleaned and pressed work clothes, playing cards and drinking bitter coffee and Amaretto.

I got some very dirty, suspicious looks from these gentlemen until Uncle Pee Wee came in behind me.

"Nicky, come with me, boy; it's good to see you."

We weaved our way between the tables and through a door at the back of the room.

"Due espresso," Uncle said just before he closed the door behind us. The room was large, some fifteen by

12

twenty, dominated by a large Swedish Empire desk in mahogany with gilded winged sphinxes for legs. The rug was Bijar. Oil paintings of hillsides, sunsets, and seascapes covered most of the walls. I settled down gingerly into a throne-style side chair of carved rosewood. Uncle was a collector. Of many things.

He took off his suit coat, draped it carefully over the back of the chair behind his desk, then sat down. A waiter brought in a tray with two small, steaming espresso cups. Uncle waited until we were alone before he spoke.

"Tell me what happened," he said.

"I was at the track that day. I saw Johnny earlier. We spoke briefly. I went to the men's room, and heard the beeper. Then I saw him. He was dead. His neck was broken. The knife from his cane was still in his hand. There was blood on the knife, but no sign of any wounds on Johnny."

"Good, then it's the bastard's own. At least he got a taste of the blade. Did you see anyone?"

"No. No one. I took the beeper. He was still wearing his raincoat."

"Yes, yes," he said, then paused for a sip of the coffee. "The police questioned me, of course. He had twenty thousand dollars in the coat. It was all still there."

I finished my coffee and stood up. "I saw your last message on the recorder. Five grand on number six in the fifth race. There must have been some very heavy last-minute betting on Trish's Lamb Chop."

He leaned back in his chair, studying me over the rim of his cup. We had a pretty good relationship, but since my parents died I hadn't see him much, unless it was around Christmas or on our birthdays.

"Do the police know you found Johnny?"

"No."

"Why did you take the beeper?"

"I'm not really sure. It was probably a mistake, though I don't see how it could help the police in their investigation." I took a sip of the coffee. "He just looked so . . . so, I don't know what to say, so violated. An old man with his neck broken. The beeper looked out of place. I guess it made him look like a crook. Maybe that's why I took it."

"I consider it a great favor, Nicky, and I appreciate it. I did not get a lot of action on that horse myself. But another bookie did. And a casino in Reno got burned very badly."

"Who were the big winners?"

"I haven't received that information yet."

"What do you hear about the race?"

He shrugged his shoulders. "Nothing. I would like it looked into, but, unfortunately, Johnny's death has created some problems. The police are being persistent in their questions. I can't ask around myself. Would you be interested?"

"I took the beeper because I didn't think it would help the police. I wouldn't want to find out who was responsible and then learn that they had been found shot to death or woke up to find horses' heads on their beds."

He laughed, and whenever he did that he reminded me of my father. "Nicky, you see too many movies. You know that kind of thing doesn't happen anymore, and I was never connected with people that did do those kinds of things. I'm a businessman, that's all, and I'd like to find out what went wrong. Anything you turn up that would lead to whoever killed Johnny, I would expect you to tell the police."

"All right then, I'll see what I can do."

He opened a desk drawer and took out a checkbook.

"Don't bother, Uncle. I've already been paid. I bet the six horse after I saw your message on the beeper."

He sat back and sighed. "Ah, Nicky, there are times when you think more like your uncle than like your father."

4

Uncle Pee Wee was wrong about the police not bothering with me. There were two cars, one unmarked, the other a black-and-white, parked in front of my flat.

Two uniformed officers got out of the black-and-white. They did it just as they were taught to at the academy, one got behind me, while the other approached me from the side. Both had their hands on the butts of their holstered guns.

"Mr. Polo?" the one coming at me from the side asked. He had his hat pushed back on his head, and a mass of blonde curls drooped down almost to his eyebrows.

I stopped and made sure my hands were visible and well away from my coat jacket.

"Yes. What can I do for you, Officer?"

"Just a few words, sir. Would you come over to the car?"

At least they were being polite. I caught sight of the

omnipresent Mrs. Damonte peeking out at us through her curtained windows.

As I got close to the radio car, the cop behind me said, "Hands on the top of the car, please."

I leaned against the top of the radio car and spread my legs. The pat down was thorough. "Mind if I ask what the hell this is all about?"

"Can we see some ID, sir?"

"Sure." I dug my wallet out and handed it to him. "What's your name, Officer?"

"Nofziger. My partner is Piombo."

Piombo must have been the strong, silent type. So far he hadn't said a word.

"I used to be one of you," I said, "a few years back."

"Yes, sir, we know," said Nofziger, handing me back my wallet. "Turn around please, sir."

I did and he snapped a pair of handcuffs on me. So much for professional courtesy.

A tall, gangly guy with a narrow, gloomy face, jutting jaw, and barbed-wire eyebrows got out of the unmarked car and sauntered over as if he had all the time in the world. "Thanks, Officers," he said. "You can put him in my car." He was wearing a dark brown, shiny polyester suit, yellow shirt, and tie that looked like it had every flower grown in the state on it somewhere. His shoes were heavy black brogues, the laces untied. "I don't think the handcuffs will be necessary," he said in a voice that seemed to come up from his socks.

Ah, professional courtesy at last. Or more likely something as unoriginal as the good guy–bad guy approach. I couldn't blame him, I'd used the same routine when I was a cop myself. It's amazing how even the most ring-wise cons will fall for it. Still, it did feel good having the cuffs taken off. When my hands were free I gave Mrs. D. a reassuring wave. She shook her head, and I wasn't sure if it was in happiness or disappointment.

"My name is Sergeant Eller," Shiny Suit said. "Alameda County Sheriff. Hop in." He even opened the car door for me.

We rode a couple of blocks in silence.

"Nice car," I said.

"Piece of shit, but the county's having financial problems, so what can you do? You know Bob Tehaney?"

"Very well." Tehaney was a homicide inspector with the San Francisco Police Department.

"So do I. I called him and checked you out, otherwise I'd have given you the Miranda, left the cuffs on you, and dumped you in county jail for the night."

"Look, Eller, I appreciate this, but you can stop trying to play the tough, hard-working, good-guy cop and just tell me what this is all about."

"It's about your fingerprints, Polo. I heard you were at the track, and I found them on the nice clean metal stall of the toilet in the Turf Club at Golden Gate Fields."

He took a right on Broadway, went through the tunnel, then turned left on Polk, against a red light. Cops are the same everywhere I guess.

"I was at Golden Gate Fields the day Johnny Aiello was killed, Eller. And I used the rest room in the Turf Club, I'm sure a lot of people did. There must have been dozens of different fingerprints."

"You'd think so, wouldn't you? But there wasn't, Polo. Oh, some from a guy named Nicholson who found the body and called the police, and one of an ambulance

18

attendant who got there before we did, but no one else's. Not even Aiello's. I talked to the janitor. Said he cleaned the room that morning, before the races started."

He made a couple more right turns while I was trying to figure out just what it was that I touched in the rest room.

"Hamburger, or just coffee?" Eller asked as he pulled the car to a stop in a McDonald's parking lot.

"Coffee, black."

He got out of the car, then came back leaning his head in through the window. "Don't go away now, okay?"

Eller came back with two hamburgers, a milk shake, a couple of baskets of fries, and my lone coffee.

"Damn," he said between mouthfuls of his burger, "this working overtime is the shits. The money's good, but I'm getting too old for it."

Eller looked to be a hard fifty, but then a lot of cops look fifty who haven't seen forty yet.

"I can give you the name of a witness that I was with at the track that day. Jane Tobin, a reporter for *The Bulletin*."

He handed me a pen and a notebook. "Write down the name. I'll have to check it out." He took a swig of his shake, leaving a thin vanilla mustache over his upper lip. "Mind taking your coat and shirt off?"

"This is hardly the time or place to get romantic, Eller."

"This Johnny Aiello, you knew him, right?"

"Yes, I haven't seen much of him in twenty years, but I knew him."

"He works for your uncle, the bookie, right?"

"I don't know. I know he has in the past."

Eller wiped his lip with a napkin, then attacked the

second hamburger. "He was, up until the time of his death, believe me. You know about his cane?"

"I know he used one."

"One of those fancy sword canes, like you see in the old movies. Never saw a real one before this. Aiello used it before he died. From the amount of blood on the knife, he must have cut somebody pretty good."

I took off my coat and unbuttoned my shirt.

"Roll the sleeves up, will you?"

I did.

He grunted. "He could have cut you in the legs, huh?"

"If you think I'm going to drop my pants in this parking lot, you're crazy, Eller."

He chuckled. "No need. I told the boys who patted you down to check you out. Crime lab says Aiello's blade went in a good inch. No way to hide a cut like that."

"Was there any blood around the body?"

"Just a few drops. We figure it dripped off the blade. Blood type was AB-negative."

"I'm A-positive."

"That's what it says on your rap sheet, but I thought I'd double check. How'd you like prison?"

"It was different."

"Did you see anyone when you were in the bathroom?"

"No."

"But you saw Aiello at the track before he was killed?"

"Right. At the paddock. I introduced him to Jane Tobin, the lady I was with."

"Aiello died as a result of his neck being broken. But

the coroner found traces of scopolamine hydrobromide in his blood."

"Knockout drops?"

"Yeah. There was a puncture wound on his right arm." He jumbled his empty milk shake cup and hamburger wrappings and tossed them out the window. "You want a ride back to your place?"

"No thanks," I said, opening the door and trying to get out without looking like I was hurrying.

Eller hit the ignition switch and gunned the car's motor. He gave me a lopsided smile and said, "It's a good thing you know Inspector Tehaney, Polo. I ain't got much use for bent ex-cops. Watch yourself."

The car squealed around in a tight U-turn and took off up Van Ness.

I made my way through the Golden Arches and went in search of a cab.

5

I was back at Golden Gate Fields early the next morning. The track itself was closed, or "dark," as the regulars like to say, but there were dozens of horses being given workouts around the track.

According to the racing form, Trish's Lamb Chop was owned by something called the Alta Group. The trainer was listed as Donald Jepson, and the jockey had been Hector Alvera.

Trish's Lamb Chop had run six races prior to her big win the day Aiello was killed, and she had never come in better than fourth. No wonder she went off at such high odds.

A small man in Levi's, a plaid shirt, and a straw cowboy hat was leaning against the rail with a stopwatch in his hand.

"I'm looking for Hector Alvera," I said, resisting the urge to throw a *partner* on the end of the sentence.

He looked my way long enough to spit a wad of tobacco juice down toward his boots. "Ain't seen him."

"How about Don Jepson?"

"Ain't seen him neither."

"Know where I might find them?"

Another shot of tobacco juice landed near his boots. "Somewhere else."

"Were you born this miserable, or did you have to work on it?" I said, wondering just how far he could reach with a spray of juice if he set his mind on it.

He grinned, showing teeth as dark as the tobacco wad stuck between them.

"What do you want them for?"

I showed him the police inspector's badge I never bothered to turn in when I left the department. "It's about the murder the other day."

"That bookie?" he asked.

"Right."

More tobacco juice ended up on the ground. "Kinda funny a bookie gettin' killed at a racetrack."

"Hilarious. You must have loved World War II."

"Korea was my war, buddy, and it weren't funny at all. I meant strange, you know what I mean. What you want to see Alvera and Jepson for?"

A big gray horse went galloping by, and the man waved at the jockey, circling his hand over his head as if he were swinging a lariat. "Bring him in, Kenny, that's enough," he said, then turned to me. "You know much about horses, Mr. Policeman?"

"I know they can hurt you, in more ways than one."

He grinned again, flashing those brown teeth. I'd

have to try and not say anything funny. One more look at those incisors and I would have to pass on lunch.

"Alvera ain't been around today. Wasn't here yesterday either. I had some work for him, but he didn't show up."

"What about Jepson?"

"Ain't seen him either. If he ain't here, you can usually find him at his place over there."

He pointed a finger in the general direction of San Francisco.

"Where there?"

"He's got a little ranch down in Woodside. That's where he keeps his horses, boards others. Owns a bar there too, The Whipcord."

Jepson wasn't listed in the telephone book. Woodside is some thirty miles south of San Francisco. It's one of those "Why didn't I buy down there ten years ago?" places. Little shacks on half acres used to go for next to nothing. Now the shacks were being knocked down and large homes with pools and stables were going in. You just had to have a stable. There were signs all over the place showing that "Horses Have the Right of Way." Kids rode to school on horseback. People got married on horseback. Housewives went shopping on horseback. If someone ever invents a saddle capable of accommodating two horny people, he'll make a fortune selling them in Woodside.

The county seat is in Redwood City. I stopped at the assessor's office and found a listing for a parcel of land under Jepson's name on Dallera Road.

It was a beautiful afternoon. I rolled the car window down and inhaled the country air. The hills were covered with oak trees, Scottish broom, and poppies. Hawks circled the blue sky slowly, while smaller birds darted in and out of the woods, doing their Air Force Blue Angels routines.

I found Jepson's place. It had a whitewashed fence stretching across the front, in the middle of which was an anchor chain-metal gate. There was a padlock on the gate. A big German shepherd came bounding down to greet me. He didn't look friendly.

I beeped the car's horn and waited. Then beeped it some more and waited some more. The dog growled every time I got close to the gate. Any attempts at being chummy with it, like, "Hi, boy," how you doing, big fella?—that kind of thing—only brought longer and deeper growls.

I gave up and went back to the car and drove to downtown Woodside. The pimply-faced kid at the gas station gave me directions to the Whipcord.

It was an old clapboard affair on the east side of the 280 Freeway. There was a hitching post running the length of the building. Two horses were tied up at the post, and about twenty motorcycles leaned up against it. The parking lot was filled with pickup trucks that looked like they worked for a living.

I expected country and western music, but all I could hear as I parked the car was loud rock.

Believe it or not, there were swinging doors leading inside. Rodney Dangerfield or Henny Youngman could have done a whole routine on the place. There were half a dozen guys in full cowboy gear and at least twenty guys in Hell's Angels–style leather, with chains, bandoliers stuffed with what looked like real bullets, and eighty pounds of hair a man. They looked like the kind of guys that thought rape was foreplay. The dining area was under

the "No Spitting" sign. I'm not saying the cocktail waitresses were rough looking, but every night they had a
starched T-shirt contest. With every third drink, they
gave you a free tattoo. That's the kind of place we're talking about, and there I was standing at the door in my blue
blazer, neatly pressed slacks, button-down shirt, and
shoes with cute little tassels on them. I'm telling you, I
just wasn't getting no respect.

I would have backed out but I was afraid they'd take
that as a sign of weakness and follow me. I walked over to
the bar. The bartender looked like a retired nose tackle
who had gone on an eating binge. He was wearing dirty
jeans and a leather vest that wasn't buttoned, and even if
it were, it couldn't keep in the pair of fifty-six double d's
drooping down toward his stomach. His head was shaved
and he was wearing a big silver earring in his left ear. I
know there are rules about that, one side for straight, one
side for gay, but I can never get it right, and this didn't
seem to be the time to ask about it.

"Give me a beer," I said in a voice that I hoped
sounded like John Wayne's.

"Regular or light?" he asked, in a surprisingly soft
voice.

"Regular's fine."

He brought me a bottle of Bud and a glass that had
more fingerprints on it than the windows of Dolly Parton's
dressing room.

I took a sip from the bottle. "Don Jepson around?"

"Who wants to know?"

Decision time. If I took out the old police badge
there would probably be a stampede to the front door and
I'd get trampled. Or one of the gorillas in leather might
want to start a game of kick the cop.

26

I put a twenty on the bar. "I'm interested in buying one of his horses."

He jerked a hand the size of a catcher's mitt toward the back of the bar. "In the office."

I picked up my beer and weaved through the crowd. A young woman in what once was a white T-shirt wouldn't move an inch, so I had to brush past her to get by. Her nipples were so sharp I was afraid they might cut my coat.

I opened the door the bartender had pointed to and found myself in a small hallway. A door straight ahead had the word *Office* printed on it in pencil. I knocked and went in. A thin, serious-faced man was sitting behind a desk counting a pile of money. He pulled the pile closer to him, like a poker player raking in his winnings.

"What do you want?" he said.

"That part of the money you won on Trish's Lamb Chop?"

"Who the hell are you, mister?"

"Didn't you think that they would start an investigation after a payoff like that? Especially when a murder's involved?"

He stood up. He was taller than I thought, well over six feet; thin, but he looked like he had a steely strength about him. He was wearing a blue checked shirt with snaps instead of buttons. The sleeves were rolled up, showing powerful wrists. His hair was gray and cut short and close to his head. He had a thick salt and pepper mustache that curled over his upper lip. A straw cowboy hat hung from a peg on the wall.

He strode over to the door, poked his head out, then shut it with a bang and turned the lock.

"I asked who you were, mister," he said, sitting

27

down in his chair again, leaning back, and folding his arms across his chest.

I tossed one of my business cards down in front of him. He leaned forward to read it, then snorted. "The people at the track hire you?"

"They wanted someone private. That way they think they can keep the state and feds out of it."

"State and feds?"

"You fix a horse race, you'd be surprised at the rules you're breaking."

"Who says I fixed a horse race?"

"Let me explain the facts of life to you, Jepson. Trish's Lamb Chop never got a smell of a win until that day, then she goes wire to wire without losing a breath. A lot of money was bet on that horse. The people at a certain casino in Nevada are upset about the losses. And they're upset that one of their people was killed before he could do anything to drop the odds down."

"Yeah, too bad about old Johnny. He wasn't a bad guy." He picked up my card and flicked the edge with his fingernail. "You're not working for the track, are you?"

"No."

"Polo." He pronounced it slowly, as if there were *w*'s in it. "That's a dago name, isn't it?"

"We prefer *Italian*."

"You telling me you work for the Mafia?"

"That's another word we don't like to use, Jepson."

"I'm telling you I didn't have nothing to do with any fixed race."

"What about your jockey?"

"Alvera? He's not my jockey. I use him when I have to, but he's not my first choice."

"But he always rode Trish's Lamb Chop. No one's

seen him for a couple of days. Know where I can find him?"

"He's probably chained to a bed with some blonde, kinky little bastard."

"Where does he live?"

"Who knows with jockeys? They move around like gypsies."

"Tell me about the horse's owner, the Alta Group."

He took a battered pack of Marlboros from his shirt pocket, shook out a cigarette, and stuck it in his mouth. I'd have bet heavy odds he'd light the kitchen match with his thumbnail, but he disappointed me, scratching it across the desk to get it started.

"Don't know much about them. They send the horse to me for boarding and training. Send me checks. I tell them when the horse is ready to race. That's about it."

"Who's they?"

"I deal with an attorney, Sam Vickers. I don't know any of the other principals."

There was a pounding at the door.

Jepson quickly shuffled all the money on the desk together and stuffed it in one of the desk drawers before going to the door.

"Who is it?" he said.

"Leo."

Jepson opened the door and the bartender was standing there. If he'd wanted to come inside, he'd have had to slide in sideways.

"Trouble," Leo said.

If there was some kind of trouble that Leo couldn't handle, I didn't want to stay around and see what it was.

"Is there a back door out of here, Jepson?"

"Yeah, down the hall. Takes you right out to the parking lot."

"There are some things we should discuss, Jepson."

He looked nervously from me to the hulking bartender. "Yeah, there are. I get out of here around seven-thirty. Come to my place, 1919 Dallera Road, around eight o'clock."

6

I pointed my clunker back toward San Francisco. What the car lacks in looks, it makes up for in conveniences. The main convenience is that it looks so much like an unmarked police car that I can park it in red zones, white zones, in front of fire hydrants, even on sidewalks, and the odds are better than two to one that I won't get a traffic tag.

It's a beige two-year-old Ford, with the required number of dings, scratches, and dents. It has a huge whip antenna, a spotlight, and one of those red "Kojak" lights that you can stick on the roof, but for my purposes just sits on the seat next to me. There's a microphone that looks very professional, but, since it's attached under the dash with Scotch tape, is not very useful. I keep a clipboard with old stolen-auto hot sheets visible on the back seat for that added touch of authenticity.

The passenger seat headrest has been hollowed out,

and there's a .38 revolver resting in there. All in all, the perfect urban vehicle for our times.

I wasn't paying any attention to the speedometer, my mind was on just how nervous Don Jepson had been during our interview. The fact that he claimed that he did all his business with the Alta Group through attorney Sam Vickers was interesting. Vickers was one of the more prominent corporate attorneys in San Francisco. It was hard to figure him being involved in anything as sordid as a fixed horse race, much less murder.

A siren brought me back to the present. A California Highway Patrol car was directly behind me. I glanced at the dash and saw I was up to almost eighty miles an hour. He came alongside, motioned his hand for me to slow down, smiled, waved, and was on his way. That's what I mean about conveniences. The jalopy not only fooled parking meter maids, but CHP officers too.

There was a message on my answering machine from Jane Tobin.

I called her at the *Bulletin*.

"You bastard," she started out sweetly. "In case you forgot, I work for a newspaper. And the only way I find out about your being questioned by the police in that Aiello man's murder is when a homicide detective visits me."

"When I confess, I'll give you an exclusive."

"Right now there's nothing I'd like more. I feel like a fool. I was with you at the track that day. A murder's committed and I don't even have an inkling for a story. And I'm with one of the prime suspects."

"You're a columnist now, way above all these low-life crime stories. Is that what Eller called me? A prime suspect?"

32

"No, but he didn't mention anyone else's name." Her voice lowered a few notches. "I didn't tell Eller about the fact that you seemed distracted after the fifth race. Or that you came back from making a bet with your fly wide open, which, unless you're a flasher, would mean that you just came back from the men's room in a distracted frame of mind."

"What's a little flashing between friends. Besides, I was told that it pays to advertise."

"This is serious, Nick. We should talk. What are you doing tonight?"

"I've got a business meeting down the peninsula. Probably won't be back until eleven."

"Stop by my place. I'll wait up for you."

"Should I bring a toothbrush?"

"The way things are going, maybe you should bring an attorney," she said, severing the connection before I could get a last word in.

The jalopy's spotlight came in handy down in Woodside as I drove down the dark, winding dirt and gravel road looking for Jepson's gate. I finally found it a little after eight. It was wide open. I drove through. The road went up a sharp incline, then started down just as sharply. A modest-sized ranch-style home stood next to a clump of eucalyptus trees. There were several lights on in the house. A barn and stalls were situated behind the house. It was so quiet, the only sounds were the crunching of the tires over the gravel. I parked next to a dust-covered red pickup and beeped my horn.

No welcoming voices. No dog barking. I beeped several times more and got the same results. Zip. Maybe that big shepherd had something about barking at night. But maybe not about biting after dark. I punched the passenger side headrest and retrieved the .38 revolver, slipped it in my pocket, and got out of the car cautiously. If this were a movie, the sound track would start to get scary: The violins would be screeching and the drums would start picking up the tempo. A painted gray wooden porch led to the front door, which was wide open; the screened door in front of it gave a view inside. I punched the doorbell and yelled for Jepson.

I took the gun out of my pocket and opened the screen door, yelling every few seconds, "Jepson, where are you?"

A sunken living room was crowded with heavy, dark furniture. The walls were covered with boldly patterned Indian blankets. There was a smoke-stained brick fireplace against one wall and a firewood storage area framed with Douglas fir timbers next to it.

The dining room had an oak table, the top circle-scarred from years of forgotten coffee cups and highball glasses. A bottle of Jack Daniels and a glass with an inch or so of the bourbon sat alongside a racing form on top of the table.

The house smelled of dust, cigarette smoke, dog hair, and neglect. A hallway led to two rooms, one with a king-sized bed that looked like it hadn't been made up in weeks. The other was nothing more than a large storage closet, with saddles, trophies, and boxes stuffed with clothing scattered around.

I checked the bathrooms. Nothing unusual there. The kitchen stove had a pot of coffee on it. The pot was cold. Food that looked like it had been there for a while was congealing on plates in the sink.

The kitchen had a back door that led out to the barn

34

and stables. I could hear the sound track in my mind picking up again. Then I heard something else. Whimpering. Low, terrified whimpering.

The barn was the kind you see in all the movies, with a hayloft on top. There was a small tractor and some tools I had never seen before neatly clamped to the wall.

The whimpering got louder as I approached the horse stalls. There was a row of them, the same dirty white color as the fence, with Dutch half-doors, the bottoms closed. There were lights strung along the outside of the stalls, the wire exposed and bare bulbs lighting up the doorway to each stall. A horse whinnied loudly as I approached the first stall, scaring the hell out of me. I peeked in. A handsome black horse stared back at me with unblinking eyes. I moved down, not bothering to look in the next three stalls. The whimpering sound was coming from the fifth one. It got louder as I got closer. I stuck my head over the bottom half-door and a big chestnut reared up and whinnied, pounding his hooves down to the ground with terrible force. His eyes looked wild and he backed to the rear of the stall and reared up again. There was a lump that once was a human being curled up against the back wall. Lying next to it was the German shepherd I'd seen that morning. He was doing the whimpering.

I checked out the adjoining stall and saw it was empty, then went back and quietly unlocked the door to the stall with the nervous chestnut. As soon as the lock was free I banged the door open, yelled as loud as I could, then ran back to the empty stall, diving over the half-door.

The horse bolted for freedom, and when I was sure he was far enough away, I ran back and entered the stall,

35

closing and locking the door behind me, in case he got homesick and wanted to come back.

The shepherd stopped whining and started growling as I approached. I crouched down on my toes and inched toward the body, all the time muttering, "nice boy, good boy," in a soft voice.

The body was wearing blue jeans and a blue checked shirt. Both were splattered with blood. The dog snapped out at me as I went to touch Jepson. I pulled my hand back in time and inched my way back outside. There was no need to check for Jepson's pulse. Most of the back of his head was gone.

7

I rang the bell to Jane Tobin's apartment. Her sleepy voice came over the intercom.

"Who is it?"

"Nick."

"You jerk, what the hell time is it?"

"About twenty after one."

"Go away."

"If I do, you'll miss a hell of a story."

"You kidding me?"

"Nope."

"You better not be. Come on up."

She buzzed me in and I took the elevator to the ninth floor. She greeted me with a tightly belted robe and a sour look. The look gradually changed as I told her the story:

After backing out of the stall, I had called the police. I waited for them in the living room, staring longingly at the bottle of Jack Daniels, though, under the circumstances, I didn't want to risk touching anything. The San Mateo County Sheriff showed up in the form of three squad cars. Later Lieutenant Gabe Gallegos appeared, and I told him the same exact story I had told the uniformed officers: I had an appointment with Jepson, the house was all lit up, I eventually found him in the stable.

The crime lab people showed up, along with the animal humane society. The dog was found to have a broken leg and several broken ribs, so he wasn't only whimpering over loss of his owner. They finally had to shoot him with a knockout dart to get to Jepson's body.

There was no doubt of the murder weapon. You could see the outline of the horse's hooves on parts of Jepson's body. They called in the voluntary mounted patrol, and finally found the horse. He was being examined under the influence of a knockout dart when Gallegos let me go.

"And that's it?" Jane said.

"There was a whip lying among the hay. It had blood on it. The poor horse had some welts that no doubt came from the whip."

She was scribbling all this down furiously on a spiral note pad while I sipped away at some of her bourbon.

"I'm going to call this into the paper," she said, standing up and heading for the bedroom.

"My name stays out of it," I said. "For now."

She nodded. "For now."

I settled back on the couch and closed my eyes, opening them every couple of minutes to take a sip of the whiskey.

When Jane finally came back, she had combed her hair, put some lipstick on, and her robe tie wasn't really so tight. She flopped down next to me.

"You seem to attract more than your fair share of dead bodies, Nick Polo."

"And one gorgeous live one." I reached over and nuzzled her neck and undid the robe tie. We kissed slowly at first, then harder. She was naked under the robe, and I started a trail of kisses from her neck, to her shoulder, down to her perfectly formed breasts. I took a hardened nipple into my mouth, sucking lightly, then moved to her other breast.

"Bless your mother for having the job done right," I mumbled as my tongue worked its way to her belly button.

"I shower first, you cook, I do the dishes," Jane commanded as she slid out of bed.

She was one of those cheerful, full-of-life, isn't-it-a-wonderful-world? types when she woke up in the morning.

I stumbled into the kitchen, got the coffee going, and went down to the lobby and got the *Bulletin*. The story wasn't all that big and exciting. It must have been added on to make the morning edition; it was listed on page fifty-four, near the obituaries:

Horse Trainer Killed on His Ranch
The body of Donald Jepson, fifty-six, well-known racehorse trainer, was found in an empty horse stall on his ranch in Woodside early this morning. The nature of his wounds leads police to believe that he was attacked by one of his horses. Jepson's dog, who was also wounded, was found lying alongside his owner, and police had to call in the Humane Society to immobilize the dog with a

39

knockout dart before they could examine Mr. Jepson's body.

Police state that they will have to wait for the coroner's report to determine the exact cause of death.

That last part was nice, it looked like the cops leaked the story rather than me.

The coffee was ready by the time Jane got through with her shower.

"Not exactly a Pulitzer, but thanks for keeping my name out of it."

I handed her the paper, took a quick shower, then checked out the refrigerator. Eggs, cheese, bread, olives. Just the basics.

I whipped a little water into the eggs, grated the cheese, and made a couple of omelets.

"Ummm," she said. "This is good. I usually just have cornflakes. Where did you learn to cook?"

"I'm Italian. It comes natural. We're all good cooks and great singers."

"Then you must have been in the shower with someone else. That wasn't exactly Sinatra I heard singing in there a while ago. What are you going to do next?"

"Sit back and have another cup of coffee while you do the dishes. Then I have a command performance with the San Mateo Sheriff."

Lieutenant Gallegos was waiting for me in his office. Sergeant Eller of the Alameda Sheriff's Department was with him, sitting in a hard-back chair, one leg crossed over the other. His shoes were untied again.

Gallegos was of medium height, with dark, thinning hair and a face that looked like it was used to smiling a lot.

40

He extended a hand. "Thanks for coming, Mr. Polo. I believe you have already met Sergeant Eller."

Eller grunted a greeting.

Gallegos handed me a typed document. "This is the statement you gave us last night. Take a look and see if it's all right as is. Any changes you want made, just write them in the margin and I'll have the secretary correct it."

I went through the three double-spaced typed pages. "Looks okay to me, Lieutenant." I took a pen from a stand on his desk and signed my name to each page.

"What were you doing down at Jepson's place?" said Eller.

"We had a business meeting at eight. I had spoken to him briefly earlier yesterday afternoon at a bar he owns. The Whipcord."

"That's a bucket of blood now," Gallegos said. "Used to be a pretty straight place, but the motorcycle gangs took a liking to it. We're called in there all the time to break up fights."

"What kind of business did you have with Jepson?" Eller asked.

"Horse business."

"Horseshit." Eller stood up and marched over to me. He had maybe an inch on me, and he had a habit of rising and falling on his feet, as if to strengthen his calves. "Aiello's a bookie. He gets killed at the track. You're there. Jepson's there too, and his horse happens to be running, a long shot. The horse wins, just about the time that Aiello gets his neck broken. Then you show up at Jepson's house and find him dead. It's connected, Polo, and you know it, and you're going to tell us about it right now."

"You think the horse somehow snuck up to the

41

bathroom and killed Aiello before the race, Sergeant? Because from what I saw last night, it looked to me that Jepson was killed by a horse."

"No doubt about that," interjected Gallegos. "Coroner confirmed it." He searched through a mess of papers scattered across his desk, found the one he wanted, and read from it. "It also shows that Jepson's blood alcohol was .21."

Point ten could get you arrested for drunk driving in this state, so Jepson had been really bombed.

"I still want to know what you were seeing Jepson about, Polo," Eller said.

"A friend wants to get into the racing game. He was a well-known trainer, that's all."

"Sure you didn't tell him that you were a Mafia man and you were pissed because he had thrown a race, and you and your friends lost a bundle?"

I felt the ground shake under me a bit. If Eller, or Gallegos, or some federal agency had Jepson under surveillance, and they had monitored our conversation, I was up the proverbial creek without a paddle.

"Mafia? Give me a break, Eller. You know the Mafia isn't active out here, and if they were they wouldn't use a small-time private detective to run their errands."

"Your uncle Dominic is connected, asshole, and you know it."

It had been so long since I had heard my uncle called anything but "Pee Wee," it took a moment for me to figure out who he was talking about.

"You're full of shit, Eller," I said, a little hotter than I should have. "You need me for anything else, Lieutenant Gallegos?"

"You're free to go as far as I'm concerned."

I started for the door.

"Any good will you had coming from your friendship with Bob Tehaney has been used up, asshole," Eller shouted as I went out the door.

I cursed myself silently in the elevator and on the way out to the car. It was stupid to blow up like that at Eller. That was just what he wanted. He won that round easy. How the hell did he know about my conversation with Jepson? Who would have had him under surveillance? Had he been throwing races on a regular basis? The thought of the feds having a tape sent shivers through my body. It didn't sound right. If Eller had a tape, or direct knowledge of one, he'd have come down a lot harder. It was probably the gorilla bartender at the Whipcord. What the hell was his name? Leo. He had been outside the door to Jepson's office. He probably overheard everything. Eller must have interviewed him. Maybe it was silly to use the threat of the Mafia with Jepson, especially since there really was almost no real Mafia connection in San Francisco.

The legends are that in the old days, when the boys came to town on the train, there were two or three big, broad-shouldered Irish cops waiting for them. A cup of coffee, then back on the train. That was the legend. The Irish ran the town in the old days all right: the papers, the police department, all the clout where it counted. The McDonough brothers ran a bookie establishment right over their bail bonds shop on Kearny, just a couple of blocks from the old Hall of Justice. Prostitution was all over the place, especially Chinatown. But the Chinese ran their own shops and their own drugs.

The Mafia did some small business in the labor organization, and it was heavy in the porno area, but most of

43

the porno came out of Los Angeles, so the Bay Area was small potatoes. Jimmy "The Weasel" Fratianno, "The Mafia Canary," had been headquartered in the city for years, but all of his "hits" had been made somewhere else. He had scratched along at tries at legitimate businesses, always trying to get into Vegas, where the real money was. *Look* magazine had tried to paint former mayor Joseph Alioto with a Mafia brush, but had wound up losing a bundle in court for its efforts.

So the Mafia left San Francisco as a sort of a neutral area, where everybody could travel through without worry. It kept its dirty hands in Los Angeles and Phoenix and left the city alone.

And I had irrefutable evidence Uncle Pee Wee wasn't connected. If he was, my father would have killed him. A bookie, no big deal. Mafia, no way.

8

The horses were back running at Golden Gate Fields that day, but Hector Alvera was among the missing.

I talked to several jockeys and got nothing from them except for the fact that none of them seemed too upset about Hector not being there.

I tried the trainers and struck out there too.

That left the grooms, usually young kids who are paid nickels and dimes for feeding, exercising, and grooming the horses. They have to put up with that kind of life, which often includes sleeping in an empty stall, if they ever want to get a chance to be a jockey.

The groom that helped me was a gangly young kid with red hair that stood up on the top of his head with the stiffness of a kitchen broom. He was wearing faded denim cutoffs and no shirt. His arms, back, and chest were covered with a mottled mass of freckles. He was washing down a panting dark brown colt.

"I'm looking for Hector Alvera," I told him.

"Ain't seen him," he said, in a rough southern accent.

"It's worth a hundred bucks."

He dropped his sponge and turned to look at me. "Cash, mister."

I took two fifties from my money clip and waved them at him. He looked over his shoulder to make sure no one was within hearing distance. "I'm not sure just where he is, but I could find out later."

"How much later?"

"When I'm through here, mister. I got a lot more horses to do."

I gave him one of my cards. "Where do you think Alvera is?"

"He's with some girl called Mona. A jockey fucker. I know where her house is, but I don't know the street name or number. But I can find it, believe me."

I handed him one of the fifties. "I'll trust you with this. You call me and you get two more. You don't call and I'll be back tomorrow to get that one back. What's your name son?"

"Jack Kirby, mister, and don't worry, I'll call you. Anytime I can make a hundred and fifty bucks and screw Alvera too, ain't no way I'll pass that up." He jumbled up the fifty, pushed it in his cutoffs pocket, and went back to grooming the horse. I could hear him whistling as I walked back to the parking lot.

I went back to my flat and spent most of the afternoon trying to get an appointment to see attorney Sam Vickers. His secretary gave me the standard put off, "He's in court, I'll have him contact you."

I checked through the various Bay Area directories for the Alta Group, but found no listing.

That left it up to the mighty IBM computer. I put in the right floppy disk, which connected me with a data base located in Southern California, punched in the name *Alta Group*, and requested checks for civil filings and fictitious-name filings in San Francisco, San Mateo, Alameda, and Santa Clara, as well as a check with the state capital, Sacramento, to see if it was a listed corporation.

I tried Sam Vickers's office again, explaining that I was calling regarding the Alta Group. Vickers was still "in court and unavailable."

Jane was coming for dinner so I wandered out in the sunny streets and picked up the proper groceries. When I got back the answering machine message counter was blank.

I went back to the IBM. The requests for Alta Group were processed. My computer screen asked me whether I was ready to receive them. I answered yes, and the printer started pounding away at God knows how many words per second. Very impressive, except that all the checks came back completely negative.

I crept down the back steps leading to Mrs. D.'s garden and picked some fresh sage and basil, then enough lettuce and tomatoes and green onions for a salad.

I was trimming and pounding the veal round steaks when Jane rang the doorbell.

"Wow, this is something," she said, rushing past me only long enough to plant a wet kiss on my cheek. It was her first visit to my flat.

She looked in the front room, with it's bricked wall and what once was a state-of-the-art stereo system. The

47

invention of the compact disc had set me back. Clever devils, those retailers. Just when you think you have everything you could ever possibly need, they change the rules, stop making records, so that you have to buy those little discs and the laser-blazing machine that makes them work. Science takes another great step ahead, and our bank accounts take a giant step backward.

"You have all this place to yourself?" she said continuing her tour. "It's huge, Nick. Just huge. How many bedrooms?"

"Three, but one's my office, the other a TV room. Take the tour. I've got to get back to the kitchen."

She came in a couple of minutes later and examined me with her hands on her hips. "I'm impressed. This must cost you a fortune."

"Just the taxes. I inherited it from my folks. There's wine in the fridge and an opener in that drawer."

She popped the cork and brought me a cold glass of Chardonnay.

"What's on the menu?"

"Saltimbocca, which roughly translates as *jump in my mouth*. Veal, prosciutto, and fontina cheese and some spices."

She watched as I prepared the meat. "How's the Aiello case going?"

"Nowhere. San Mateo's sure the horse killed Donald Jepson. His blood count was .21. You'd have to have about twelve more glasses of that wine to get to that point."

"What about the horse?" she asked.

"What about the horse?"

"Will they have to kill it? Was it the horse that won the race?"

48

"Good question, newspaper lady. I don't know. I didn't get much of a chance to ask any questions. Eller, the Alameda cop who spoke to you, was there. He's not too fond of me."

"Why would someone like Jepson, who's been training horses for over twenty years and who made a good living at it, suddenly go nuts, get drunk, and start whipping some poor horse?"

"You seem to know a lot about Jepson," I said, layering the thin veal steaks with several slices of the Italian ham and cheese, then rolling them up and securing them with small skewers.

"I ran him through the paper library, and talked to Ron Taylor. He follows the horses for the paper and knew Jepson. Ron says he was top of the line for a long time, then his wife died, he remarried, apparently not well, then started hitting the bottle. Taylor said he had heard that Jepson had a few heavy battles with his new wife, but that he'd bet the house that Jepson would never use a whip on a horse."

While Jane refilled our glasses, I put a pan on the stove, waited for it to get hot, then dropped in some butter, olive oil, the sage and basil leaves, and a little Dijon mustard, then turned down the heat and dropped in the veal.

Ten minutes later we were at the table digging in. We were on our second bottle of wine when the phone and the doorbell rang at almost the same time.

I asked Jane to get the door while I picked up the phone.

"This is the operator. I have a collect call for Mr. Nick Polo from Jack Kirby. Will you accept the charges?"

Kirby. The young groom. Smart kid. He was going

to pick up a quick hundred and fifty bucks and he wouldn't pop for a fifty-cent phone call.

"Yes, I'll accept operator."

"Mr. Polo. I found him, Alvera I mean."

"What's the address?"

"914 Anderson Street, San Francisco."

"Okay, Jack, I'll check it out and drop the rest of the money off to you tomorrow."

When I hung up Jane was standing beside me.

"There's a little old lady at the door, but I can't understand a word she's saying."

Mrs. Damonte was standing outside the door with a plate of cookies. I'd forgotten it was the first of the month. She was coming to pay the rent.

Although I'm sure she can understand English, in all the years I've known her I've only heard her speak three words: nopa, shita, and her latest, bingo. So I have to speak to her in my limited Italian-Sicilian vocabulary.

"Come in Mrs. Damonte, this is Jane Tobin."

She smiled and handed Jane the plate of cookies. "She's not Italian."

"No."

"Skinny. I have a niece just come over. I introduce you."

"Nopa," I said as sternly as I could manage. "Would you like a drink?"

"Maybe small one."

I escorted her back to the kitchen. Her eyes bounced back and forth taking everything in.

Mrs. D.'s favorite was a shot of Frenet Branca, an evil-tasting liqueur bottled in Italy.

She stuck her nose over the stove and inspected the pan while I made the drink.

"You use spices from the garden?"

"They were nice." She sold spices to several of the nearby restaurants and kept an inventory on every leaf.

She took her drink, nodded to Jane, then tilted the glass back and finished it in one swallow.

Now it was time to get down to business. She opened her black leather purse, took out a coin purse, and, turning her back to Jane, began handing me ten-dollar bills reluctantly, one at a time, all the while staring at me with sad, soulful eyes. Since I could rent out the garage alone for what she was paying for her flat, she got little sympathy in return.

"Tell her the cookies are delicious," Jane said.

"She says the cookies are delicious."

"Tell her she needs to eat more," Mrs. D. said, then made her way to the front door.

When I was back in the kitchen Jane was on her third cookie. "These really are fabulous."

They were light brown, a little bigger than a teaspoon each. I popped one in my mouth. "Made out of almonds, pine nuts, sugar, flour, and egg whites. When they're ready to go in the oven, the cook presses in one edge of the cookie, supposedly to make a beanlike impression. They're called Fave dei Morti. Beans of the Dead."

Jane winced. "What an awful name for something so delicious. But what a nice lady. Does she always bring you stuff like that?"

"Only on rent day."

"What a wonderful person."

I didn't have the heart to tell her how low the rent was.

51

I got a bottle of brandy and poured two small snifters. "I have to go out," I told her.

"Why? That phone call?"

"Yes. I've got an address for the jockey, Hector Alvera."

"Where's he at?"

"With Mona, the jockey fucker."

"If you think I'm going to miss a chance to meet someone called Mona the jockey fucker, you're crazy."

9

Jane insisted on driving. She had a cute little Chrysler convertible, red, with black leather and a white top. Cute, but a convertible in San Francisco is about as useful as a refrigerator in an igloo. I think she had had the top down twice in the six months she had owned the car.

Anderson Street was located in the Bernal Heights District of San Francisco, a mishmash of stucco and wood-frame homes, some of them built right after the big quake of 1906. The streets were narrow and hilly and Jane circled the block twice looking for a parking space, finally parking right in the driveway of Mona's house, edging her way in between an old sedan with rusted fenders and a pickup with a bed full of plywood.

I really didn't have a plan, but smiled confidently at Jane as I pushed the doorbell.

We didn't have long to wait. The door was opened by a rail-thin, dark-haired man with one of those dark skinny cigars Gilbert Roland always smoked in the movies, stuck between his teeth. A lightweight jockey is 110 pounds, middle 110 to 113, and anything over that is a heavyweight. The most they can weigh is 117. Whatever this little guy weighed, it was all muscle. He was completely naked. He had a big nickel-plated revolver in his right hand and an enormous hard-on. Both were pointed right at me.

"What the fuck do you want?" he said.

"Hector?"

"Who wants to know?"

"We're from next door," I said, grabbing Jane by the elbow and pulling her to me. "Friends of Mona. We heard you were having a party. My girl friend wants to join you."

He had a big, droopy Pancho Villa mustache that stayed pointed down even when his lips moved up in a smile.

"Come in then," he said in a slurred voice. I stepped inside, grabbed at the gun with my left hand, planted my feet, and crouched down so I was level with his head, hitting him as hard as I could with a right to the chin. The gun clattered to the floor, and he skidded along the carpet, coming to a rest when his head made contact with a purple overstuffed sofa.

"Did you have to hit him so hard?" Jane asked. "He's such a little guy."

He was lying on his back, and his pecker was sticking straight up and looked big enough to hang a flag on. "Short, maybe," I said. "Stay here and keep an eye on him."

"How could I take my eyes off him, for God's sake."

The house looked like it had been decorated by someone with an account at a flea market. There were

54

gaudy paintings on velvet, mostly of naked women with big pouts and bigger breasts. The furniture was a recent attempt to capture the Art Deco look: blond wood, plastics, and engraved glass.

I used the gun as a pointer, entering each room cautiously. The woman was in the back bedroom. The walls were covered in deep red flocked wallpaper, the chest of drawers painted in a shiny black enamel, the rug a fake zebra skin. The bed was a four-poster painted black to match the dresser. Directly over the bed the ceiling had been covered with squares of smoky-veined mirror tiles.

She was tied to the bed with black nylon rope. Over her eyes was a black sleep mask. A pair of green plastic ear protectors, the kind people wear on a shooting range, was clipped over the top of her blond hair.

I dropped the gun to my side and said, "Shit," out loud. Three bodies. Pretty soon Green Street Mortuary was going to give me finders' fees.

I touched her carotid artery and her head snapped over as she tried to bite my hand.

Jane padded alongside me and said, "Oh, my God."

"Hector," yelled the lady on the bed. "What the fuck are you up to, damn it? I'm getting tired of this shit!"

I tugged off her ear protectors and eased up the sleep mask. "Are you Mona?" I asked.

"Don't touch me, you creepy bastard. I told him nobody else unless I check them out. Untie me you asshole."

I undid her feet, letting Jane work on her hands. The rope was tied in simple slip knots.

She struggled to a sitting position. She was a big woman, large-boned, heavily fleshed, with a soft oval face and straight blond hair that hung down well past her

55

shoulders. She looked to be somewhere between thirty-five and forty. "Who are you? This is my house and I'm particular about who I let in. I told Hector that."

She went to a nearby closet and took out a bright red peignoir.

I shoved the revolver in my waistband. "My name is Polo. This is my friend Jane Tobin. She's a reporter. We're doing a story on how jockeys spend their time away from the track."

"Don't be a wise ass, mister. Where is that little prick?"

Hector might have his deficiencies, but that was hardly an accurate description, unless Mona had un-believably high standards.

"He's in the front room, asleep. He had a bad fall."

"Well he can fall right out of here, with the two of you. This is a private house, not a massage parlor."

"He's not exactly dressed for the outdoors right now."

"His crap is in there," she said pointing to the closet. She narrowed her eyes and looked at Jane. "You really a reporter, honey?"

"Yes, I am."

"Why don't you let your boyfriend dress Hector, while you and I have a cup of coffee."

Jane winked at me and followed Mona to the kitchen. I picked up Hector's clothes—jeans and a sweat-shirt and beat-up white jogging shoes—from the closet floor, and went back to the living room.

He was still lying on the floor, snoring lightly. I shook him a few times, but got no response and went to the kitchen. The girls were jabbering away, but stopped talking as I came in. "Hector needs a drink," I said.

"Beer in the fridge," Mona replied, measuring coffee from a can and pouring it into a top of a Proctor-Silex.

I took a can of Bud out to Hector and dribbled a few drops on his lips. Then a few more drops. He started to come out of it. His dark eyes blinked, then he rubbed his chin.

"Hey, man. What the fuck you hit me for?"

I dropped his clothes beside him. "Get dressed Hector. We're going for a ride." I took out his revolver and slapped the barrel against the palm of my left hand.

"Who are you, man?"

"It's about the race, Hector. We're not happy about it at all. You were dogging it with Trish's Lamb Chop those first few races. You're going to lose your license if you get out of this alive."

He stood up and flopped down on the couch, putting his pants on one leg at a time, just like the rest of us.

"Hey, man. I just did what they told me to do. They said the horse wasn't ready, don't push him, that's all. I just do what they say. I'm just the jockey, what you want me to do, man?"

"Yeah, but that last race you knew he was ready, didn't you, Hector. You bet a lot of money that race."

"No law against betting on a horse, man." He put on his shoes, then reached down for the beer can, shook it, smiled when he found it almost full, and took a long, thirsty drink.

"Who told you not to run the horse in the early races?"

"Jepson, man. Who else?"

He was up, prancing around now, his confidence coming back. The beer must have stimulated whatever else he had floating around in his bloodstream. I stuck the gun barrel under his nose.

"Jepson's dead, Hector. That leaves you holding the bag."

He took a step back and sank down onto the couch again. "Jepson's dead? You shittin' me?"

"Where have you been the last couple of days, Hector? He's dead all right. Killed by a horse. At his ranch. Someone who knew him, and horses, got him into a stall and spooked the horse. Someone like you, pal."

He bounced up again. "Not me, man. I been here all the time. You can ask Mona. I only went out a couple of times to buy some booze and . . ." He looked at me and rubbed his jaw. "You ain't really no cop, are you, mister?"

"No. But I know the cops who are handling Jepson's death, and they'd like to talk to you. The people at the track want to talk to you, and there are some guys who lost a lot of money when you galloped home with Trish's Lamb Chop. They're really anxious to talk to you. They don't like to be caught with their pants down on a fixed race."

"Jesus, man, I tell you I didn't do nothing but what Jepson told me to do."

"Who else besides Jepson gave you advice on how to run the horse?"

"No one."

"What about the horse's owners?"

"Never even heard of them, man. I don't know who owns the goddamned horse. I got paid for my rides, that's all I care about. Jepson told me to nurse the horse, take it easy with him, that he had a bum wheel. The horse looked good to me, but I ain't no trainer. They tell me to

58

hold him back, I hold him back. You don't do what they tell you, man, you never get no more rides."

"What did Jepson tell you the day you won?"

Alvera drained what was left of the beer, then shook the empty can in his hand. "He told me that the horse was ready. Really ready. Take the early lead and let him run. That's what I did man. That son of a bitch ran like Citation's ghost, man. I mean we had power to spare. It was like driving a fucking Ferrari."

"How much did you put down on the horse?"

"Nothing myself, but Jepson gave me some tickets. Fifty to win. Man, I wish they were all that easy."

I questioned him another ten minutes, but he didn't change his story. He and Jepson had a working relationship, that was all. He claimed he'd never been to Jepson's ranch, never been to his bar. "I met his old lady, the new one. Man, she would have given Mona a run for her money. What a woman. Too much for old Jepson."

I advised Alvera to contact Lieutenant Gallegos and Sergeant Eller, knowing full well he wouldn't, but at least I could tell the cops in good faith that I'd tried.

Jane and Mona were still chattering away in the kitchen. They seemed to be getting along famously.

Mona poured Alvera a cup of coffee and rustled her fingers through his hair as if she were consoling a dog who'd been naughty.

When we were in the car I asked Jane what she and Mona were talking about.

"She wants to write a book. That's one interesting woman. Do you know why she's hung up on jockeys?"

"The thrill of the ride?"

"No. Blood tests. She says that the jockeys are always getting their blood and urine tested for possible drugs. Any AIDS or herpes viruses show up. She feels that they're the safest group of men in the world."

Times were changing too fast for me. It used to be June, Moon, Spoon, I love you; dance lessons so you could sweep a girl off her feet, candy, flowers. Now all a guy had to do was get his blood checked regularly.

10

I was back at Golden Gate Fields by ten the next morning. I found Jack Kirby cleaning out a stall.

"Here's that hundred I owe you," I said.

He dropped his rake and took the cash. "Thanks. If you waited a day you could have saved your money. Alvera came in this morning. Some cop's talking to him now."

"What does the cop look like?"

"Tall, skinny guy, dark hair, weird dresser. I don't know, like a cop, I guess."

I handed Kirby two twenty-dollar bills. "This is to remind you, you never saw me."

"Saw who?" Kirby grinned, stuffing the bills in his jeans, and picking up his rake.

"What about Trish's Lamb Chop? Is he here at the track?"

"Nah, ain't been back since he won big. I don't know where he is. Probably still at Jepson's ranch."

I hotfooted it out to the parking lot, drove onto the freeway, took the University Avenue off ramp, and stopped at the first pay phone I saw.

I looked up the number for the Alameda Sheriff, and asked for homicide.

"Sergeant Eller, please."

"He's not in," said a bored voice.

"Would you tell him that Nick Polo called, and that I have an address for Hector Alvera. He can be reached at 914 Anderson Street, San Francisco."

"Will he know what this is all about?" the voice asked.

"Yes, I'm sure he will," I said, replacing the receiver, and dialing the operator for the number of the San Mateo County Sheriff's office.

Eller was no doubt going to be upset with me getting to Alvera first, and there was no telling what Hector would tell him, but at least I was on record with Eller's office for passing on the address.

Calling Gallegos was another step in covering my backside.

"I don't know if you're interested or not, Lieutenant, but Hector Alvera, the jockey who worked for Don Jepson, is living with a woman in San Francisco." I gave him the address.

"Thanks, Polo, I'll pass the word to Sergeant Eller."

"I already did."

"Really covering your ass, aren't you? What's your interest in Alvera?"

"He was riding one of Jepson's horses the day that the bookie was killed at the track. The horse was a long shot, came in, paid a lot of money. A client thought that there might have been something funny with the race."

"What did Alvera tell you?"

"That he held the horse back in the earlier races. On Jepson's instructions."

"So the race was fixed?"

"Not necessarily. Jepson told him the horse was hurting in the early races. He could have been."

"Who's your client?"

"Someone who bet on the wrong horse. Speaking of horses, the one that killed Jepson. Was it Trish's Lamb Chop?"

"No, hold on a minute." There was the clatter of the phone dropping to the desk and the rustling of papers.

"Horse by the name of Chinesey Club. I don't know how the hell they pick these names. Two-year-old. Jepson had just taken it in."

"What about Trish's Lamb Chop? Was he stabled at Jepson's place?"

"Nope." There was a long pause. Then Gallegos said, "Look, Polo. I checked you out. Got mixed reviews, but enough guys I trust say you're okay, so I'll tell you what I'm going to do. The information you gave me about Alvera was okay, and I'm going to feed you something now that will make us even. They did an autopsy on Chinesey Club. The owner wanted him put away, or to sleep, as the veterinarians say. No drugs of any kind, but the horse had been fed an unusually large amount of something called sweet mix—a combination of oats, barley, corn, and molasses. You can buy the stuff commercially at any feed store. People give it to their horses as a kind of a treat. But you give too much of it to a horse, especially a young horse like Chinesey Club, and it gets hyper, keyed up, easy to excite, you know what I mean?"

"So somebody juiced up the horse then threw Jepson in with him."

"Could be. No doubt that the horse killed him. And killed the dog, too. Vet had to put him to sleep. Now, like I say, that makes us even. What I want you to do is make us uneven. Anything you get that can help in this, I want to hear it first, okay?"

"Okay, Lieutenant, and I appreciate the information. About all I've got for you now is that the owner of Trish's Lamb Chop is something called the Alta Group. I couldn't find anything on them at all. According to Jepson, he didn't know who they were either. He got all his instructions from an attorney, Sam Vickers."

"Vickers? He's big league. I don't see him involved in any of this. He's rich enough to buy the whole damn racetrack."

"I've been trying to see him. No luck so far."

"Keep me posted," Gallegos said.

Before he could hang up, I asked, "What about Jepson's wife? Alvera said she was too much woman for him."

Gallegos laughed. "He could be right. I spoke to her. Her only concern seemed to be whether or not Jepson made out a will. While I was at the ranch she was digging through his papers, but didn't come up with anything. I talked to the uniformed boys who patrol around the Whipcord. They got the impression that it was Jepson's wife who turned the place around from quiet little cowboy bar into a motorcycle disco, or whatever the hell you'd call it now."

"Mind if I talk to her?"

"No. Like I said, just keep me posted. Her name is Connie. Lives in Daly City." He gave me her address and phone number. "Keep in touch, Polo. I somehow get the feeling that you're going to be around when the next bomb goes off."

Since I was on a hot streak with cops, I decided one more wouldn't hurt, and drove back across the Bay Bridge to San Francisco and parked under a "Police Vehicles Only" sign in an alleyway alongside the Hall of Justice.

Inspector Bob Tehaney was sitting at his desk, a damp cigarette hanging from the corner of his mouth, Humphrey Bogart style. He was past retirement age, a thin, sandy-haired man with a sour stomach and a narrow, pinched face.

"Morning, Bob," I said.

"You in more shit?" he asked.

"A lieutenant in San Mateo, Gabe Gallegos, is suddenly being very cooperative with me."

He drew deeply on his cigarette and puffed the smoke toward the ceiling. "Good guy, Gallegos. One of his kids went to Notre Dame. Pretty good basketball player."

That explained Gallegos. If Muammar Qaddafi had a kid who played for Notre Dame, Tehaney would have nominated Qaddafi for the Nobel Peace Prize.

"An Alameda cop, Eller, hasn't been very cooperative."

"Eller's an asshole," Tehaney said. "They both asked me about you. I told them the same thing. Eller's having problems with Aiello's case." He crushed out his cigarette in an overfilled ashtray and immediately lit up another unfiltered Lucky Strike. "Funny thing about your prints being the only ones around when Aiello got killed."

"Very funny." I told him about my day at the track.

"Yeah, Eller double checked your alibi with the reporter lady. He ran Aiello through Sacramento, and I checked him out for misdemeanor arrests in San Francisco. Johnny had been clean for a long time."

"Tough way for an old man to die," I said. "Eller tell you anything interesting?"

"No. He wanted to know about your uncle. He's been clean a long time, too. Didn't seem to impress Eller much."

"My uncle would be the last man in the world to want Johnny Aiello killed."

Tehaney shrugged his thin shoulders. "It's Eller's problem. I'll let him worry about it."

"Let's walk," said Dominic "Pee Wee" Polo. He was dressed in a lightweight beige suit, white shirt, and brown tie. I couldn't remember the last time I had seen him without a suit and tie. "Always dressed for business," my mother would say about him.

It was a nice sunny afternoon in North Beach. We left The Café and crossed Columbus and walked to Washington Square. The park benches were filled with a mixture of old Italian men smoking their dark Marco Petri cigars, and young men and women on their lunch breaks. A group of Chinese children were tossing a Frisbee over the head of a jumping golden retriever.

"I'm not getting very far," I said. "What have you turned up about who made the bets?"

"Let me tell you how I work, Nicky. I have a certain number of clients. The list has stayed remarkably steady

66

over the years. Someone leaves, dies, another takes his place. Always someone recommended. Someone I won't have to worry about. I'm not looking for new business. What I have is enough. Part of my responsibilities are to take care of the track, watch the bets for other businessmen like myself, you know what I mean?"

We stayed within the confines of the park, walking along the paved path. The Chinese kids' Frisbee soared by and we both stopped a minute to watch the dog try and catch up with it. "Yes, I understand, Uncle. Johnny Aiello was the stopper and bandwagon man for you."

"*Si*. But not only for me. For the others also. Some seven others here, and also for certain casinos in Nevada. Most of the time there was no need for Johnny to do anything. Most of the time if one businessman was overloaded on a certain horse, he would spread the bets around; it is a common practice. But this time the bets came in late. There was no time for anything but to have Johnny knock down the odds at the track."

"So who took the big losses?"

"One casino in Reno, the Fiesta. And someone on the peninsula. Someone rather new. Bobby North. He took a very heavy hit."

"What kind of a guy is North?"

"Like I said, new. I don't know him well. He's not," he rolled his hand around under his mouth, searching for the right word, "*capice*. Young, not too smart, but he's making money, Nicky, lots of money. He has a lot of the younger customers from the Silicon Valley."

"A yuppie bookie, just what the world needs. Was the man who placed the bet a regular?"

"Yes, North told me that at least. He wouldn't give me his name. North blames me for part of his losses. He

67

was very upset over the fact that the odds were not shortened at the track. He was . . . well, if you have to talk to him, don't be concerned if you have to be a little firm with him."

"Did he tell you how much this man bet?"

"Yes. Fifteen hundred. And five thousand was bet at the casino."

"Fifteen hundred? On the one horse? Had he ever bet anything like that before with the bookie?"

"Not on a horse. Once a thousand on a football game."

There was an open bench and we sat down under the shade of an elm tree. A glassy-eyed young man with purple spiked hair zoomed by on a skateboard, seemingly trying to get as close as possible to our outstretched feet. I did some fast calculating. Fifteen hundred at roughly twenty to one should come out to thirty thousand dollars. And a five-thousand dollar bet at the casino would bring back one hundred thousand dollars. No wonder they wanted Aiello to bring down the odds. "Do we know for sure it was the same bettor? With North and the casinos?"

He took a piece of ecru-colored paper from his suit pocket. "This is the name of the man who made the bet at the casino."

The paper showed the name James Widmer.

"I don't know if he is the same man who dealt with Bobby North, but that is the name the man used when he collected on the winning tickets at Fiesta Casino," my uncle said.

"What kind of identification did he use?"

"A driver's license. A social security card. All very legitimate."

"Where the hell is Widmer? I'd like to see him."

"I can take you to him, but you would need a shovel to see him. James Widmer died here in San Francisco three months ago."

11

Luckily, Mrs. D. never gave anything away, so I dug through the neatly stacked newspapers in the garage and found the obituary for James Albert Widmer. It showed he was survived by his parents, William and Margaret, and his sister Donna and brother Terrance.

The city directory listed a William Widmer, stock-broker, with a residence address on the 400 block of Spruce Street.

The home was a three-story, redwood-shingle affair. The woman who answered the door was somewhere in her early fifties, with frosted hair and a thin, handsome face. Though it was shady on her doorstep, she seemed to be squinting against a bright light.

"Mrs. Widmer?"

"Yes, what is it?" she asked, a little stammer in her voice.

"I'm sorry to disturb you, ma'am, but I'm an investigator. It's about someone using James's name and identification."

Her eyes narrowed. "Speaking of identification, may I see yours, please?"

I pulled out my wallet and showed her the private investigator's license issued by the State of California.

"Come in please," she said, after examining the license closely. "Sit down." She apologized for the mess, which consisted of a few magazines that were spread unevenly across the heavy gloss of a polished coffee table. The room was painted a pale green and the furniture was covered in subtle white and gray stripes.

She waited until I was seated, then said, "Now what is this about someone using my son's name?"

"Has anyone else contacted you about this, Mrs. Widmer?"

"No."

"Well, I'm afraid I'm bringing bad news. Someone used James Widmer's social security number and driver's license as identification when they placed some large bets, and won a great deal of money, in a Nevada casino."

Her hand clasped her chest. "My God, when was this?"

"Just a few days ago."

She ran a nervous hand through her hair. "Jimmy was ill, in a coma, for several months before he died, Mr. Polo. I had no idea that any of his papers were stolen. I don't know what happened to his driver's license and things like that. Really, it was something I never even thought about. Why would they use his name?"

"The casinos have to record the names of big winners, and then give the information to the Internal Revenue Service. Were any of his things ever stolen? Was there ever a robbery, or a burglary—anything like that?"

"No, not that I'm aware of. My God, what kind of a world are we living in?"

A big, broad-shouldered man in his mid to late twenties came into the room.

"What's the matter, Mom? Who's this?"

"Just an insurance man, Terry."

He was a bright, rugged-looking guy, with light blond hair and his mother's blue eyes.

I offered my hand. "Someone got ahold of some of your brother's identification papers." I explained about the bet at the casino.

Mrs. Widmer stood abruptly. "Please excuse me," she said, and walked away from us in a hurry, a handkerchief going to her eyes.

Terry Widmer gave me an appraising look. "It's been hard on Mom."

"Any idea on who might have stolen your brother's driver's license and social security number?"

"No. Hell, I don't even know where they were; here, or at the hospital, or at school."

"School?"

"Stanford. Jimmy was a junior when he got injured."

"Just what did happen to your brother?"

He rubbed his forehead, as if soothing away the pain. "Jimmy was in a car wreck. He was driving. A couple of his friends were with him. They received minor injuries. Jimmy's were major. Subdural hematoma. The skull injuries caused a constant pressure on his brain. He never woke up. Was in a coma for almost three months before he died." He managed a pale smile. "It was a blessing when he finally went. It was awfully hard on all of us, but especially my mother. There was no chance of him ever recovering, ever leading anything near a normal life if he pulled out of the coma. The brain damage was just too extensive."

"Did your brother ever do much gambling?"

"Gambling? Are you kidding? Jimmy? No way. You know what it costs to go to Stanford, Mr. Polo? My parents aren't poor, but putting us through school has been a drain on them, financially."

"You went to Stanford too?"

"Yes."

"Terry, you should tell your mother or father to get in touch with their attorney. Uncle Sam will come looking for the taxes on the money that was won at the casinos."

"I'm an attorney, I'll handle it. Thanks for the warning."

"Would you have a spare picture of your brother?"

He put his hands behind his back and pushed his lips out, as if giving great thought to my request. "Why would you want a picture of Jimmy?" he finally asked.

"Because I have a hunch whoever used his ID in Nevada was also using his name here with a bookie for the last couple of months."

Terrance Widmer stood there for several moments. His gaze seemed to turn inward, like a blind man's. "I've got one upstairs, I'll go get it."

Bobby North operated out of a small shop in an old, run-down industrial area in East Palo Alto. The faded paint on the window of the entrance door showed the name Continental Candies.

There was still half an hour or so before the sun set. I looked at my watch. My appointment with North was for

73

seven o'clock, and I was right on time. The door was locked. I knocked, and eventually it opened a crack.

"Nick Polo to see Bobby North," I said, passing one of my business cards to the sliver of face I could see on the other side of the door.

It slammed shut, and I waited a good two minutes before it opened again.

A short, balding guy with yellow slacks, a yellow shirt opened to the waist, a weight-lifter's build, and sun-worshipped brown skin scowled at me.

"You related to Pee Wee?" he asked.

"He's my uncle."

"How do I know you're who you say you are?" He spoke so fast, the sentence came out almost as one word.

"I've got an appointment with Bobby North. If he doesn't want to talk, forget about it," I said, turning on my heels and starting to walk away.

"Hey, hot head, slow down," he called to me. "I'm North but I've got to check you out."

I dug out my wallet and showed him my driver's license.

"Okay, okay, come on in."

The room was narrow and contained only a counter with a faded red formica top, a chrome cash register, and some knotty pine shelving half-filled with pink cardboard boxes on the wall. There was a wedge of light coming from a door behind the counter, and I could hear phones ringing.

"What can I do for you, Polo?" Bobby North said, leaning back against the counter. Hanging from a thick gold chain around his neck was a medallion big enough to leave a bruise.

"I want some information on the man who made that big bet on Trish's Lamb Chop the other day."

"He's a customer. I'd go broke giving away customers' names. I told your uncle that."

"You'll go broke paying off bets like that, North."

"If your fucking uncle had been on the ball and taken care of the odds at the track, I wouldn't have had to pay off so fucking much."

I smiled and moved closer to him. A thin trace of white powder showed around his left nostril.

"How many people do you have working for you in that next room, Bobby?"

"What the fuck is it to you?"

"I'd like to know, because in just a minute I'm going to start beating the shit out of you, and I'm just curious how many more goofballs you've got hiding out around here."

He laughed and shook his head, sending the medallion swinging back and forth across his chest like a pendulum. He reached out with both hands for my coat lapels.

"Listen, asshole," was as far as he got before I slammed him in the stomach with the tip of my elbow. Dangerous weapon, elbow tips: hard, pointed. The army combat training officer explained it this way to me: If a fireman takes his big axe and pounds it with all his strength against a piece of unbreakable safety glass, nothing will happen, other than maybe the axe will leave a scar on the glass surface. But you take an ice pick, make one sharp strike, the tip of the pick will penetrate and the glass will crumble like popcorn.

The theory certainly worked on Bobby North. My

75

elbow punctured all those thick stomach muscles he'd worked so hard on, his face turned pale under that terrific tan and he started to sink to the floor. I grabbed him by his shirtfront and held him up.

"You're stupid, Bobby. You're not going to be in business very long. You're sniffing coke instead of paying attention to your job. You've got a front that wouldn't fool a boy scout. I can hear the action from here."

He tried talking but nothing came out of his mouth but choking sounds.

I walked around the counter and opened the door to the back room. There were a half-dozen metal desks. A man and three women were answering phones. They all had pencils in hand and stacks of notepaper in front of them. There was a big tape recorder, the kind with the exposed tape reels, attached to each phone.

One of the women put her hand over the mouthpiece of the phone she was using. "Where's Bobby?" she asked.

"Getting his nose scratched."

She nodded and went back to her phone.

North was sitting spread-legged on the floor. I squatted down next to him.

"Who made the bet, Bobby?"

He was breathing deeply. He spoke between breaths. "You're a dead man, Polo. I'm connected."

"You're going to be connected to a pair of handcuffs if you don't learn how to handle business and be polite to people." I grabbed the medallion and yanked. "The name."

"Widmer. Jimmy Widmer."

I took the picture that Terry Widmer had given me of his brother and shoved it under North's face.

"Is this the man?"

"Nah, that's not him."

"You sure?"

"I don't pass that kind of money off if I'm not sure," he said.

"When did you pay him off?"

"The day after the race."

"Where?"

"At school."

"What school?"

He turned his eyes up and looked at me as if I had asked a stupid question.

"Stanford," he said, "Stanford University."

12

North gave me a description of the kid he'd given the money to. White, medium height, medium build, dark hair, mustache, glasses. Great description, covering only about half the male student body at Stanford.

He'd met the man he knew as James Widmer twice. Always on campus, Tressider Union, near the cafeteria. Widmer paid his bets off and picked his winnings up at North's usual drop, between noon and twelve-thirty at the cafeteria.

North couldn't remember just who had first brought Widmer to him. His code name was SU46, which meant that there were at least forty-five other Stanford University students, professors, whatever, who had accounts with North.

"He got lucky a few times on me, but I made most of it back. He played football cards, basketball games, but mostly the horses," Bobby North said, while massaging his stomach.

He made a gun out of his fist, cocking his thumb and looking at me over the barrel of his finger. "I'll be in touch with you. You can count on it."

"Don't do anything stupid, Bobby. You're fooling about as many people as you're capable of fooling right now."

He sneered, actually sneered. I wondered how many Richard Widmark flicks he had watched to get just the right look. "We'll see who's stupid."

North seemed to be the kind of guy that had to get in the last word, so I let him have it, otherwise we'd be there another hour saying things like, "So's your old man," and, "Oh, yeah?"

The address Lieutenant Gallegos had given me for Connie Jepson was on South Mayfair, in Daly City. There was a song a few years back about "ticky-tacky houses all in a row." Well, this place was that songwriter's inspiration: Westlake, a sprawling subdivision of a thousand or so houses built along the coast just south of San Francisco. The best thing you could say about the weather was that it was consistent. Consistently cold, wet, windy, and foggy. A man named Dolger had built rows and rows of single-family homes on the sand dunes in San Francisco out toward the ocean. People thought he was crazy, that no one would ever live there. He made millions. When there wasn't a sand dune left in sight, Dolger had moved south to an even more uninhabitable spot, Westlake, and again people said he was crazy. Why can't I get crazy like that? Just once.

All of the houses on the street were identical: full basements, stucco fronts, outside stairs. Each had a small lawn with, of all things, a bewildered-looking palm tree stuck in the middle.

Some old, wet newspapers littered the stairs leading to the front door of Connie Jepson's. I knocked and the door was opened with a slap.

"I thought I asked you . . ."

The woman was short, even in her cowboy boots. They were red, and so were her pants and top. She had long, jet black hair cascading down over her shoulders.

I stood there with my hand in the air, ready for another knock at the door.

"I'm sorry," she said, "I thought you were someone else." She smiled, then turned it around quickly. "Just who are you, mister?"

A small black poodle skidded to a stop alongside her.

"Nick Polo's my name, Mrs. Jepson." I showed her my old police badge. "It's about your husband."

"Oh, all right. Come in." The dog started sniffing my shoes. "Get away, Nero," she said, then turned her smile on me again. It was a nice smile. "Nero. Tough name for him, huh? I might as well have a goldfish for all the protection he's worth."

"How did he get along with your husband's German shepherd?"

"About as well as Don and I got along." Her pretty face saddened. "I was sorry they had to put him to sleep. And that poor horse. God, it was a real tragedy."

Poor dog, poor horse. Nothing said about poor Donald, her husband.

There was a small front room, and a smaller dining room. The dining room table and chairs were covered with cardboard boxes.

"I've still got a lot of unpacking to do," she said.

"Have a seat in here." She pointed to the living room. "Can I get you a cup of coffee, or something to drink?"

"A beer would hit the spot."

"I'll be right back." She strutted—that would have to be the word for that cowboy-booted walk—to the kitchen. The furnishings looked new and inexpensive, the type of stuff you'd buy for a rental unit. I sat down on a sofa covered with protective cellophane. It squeaked when I settled in. There were no paintings on the walls. No bookcases. An expensive-looking giant screen TV stood next to a high-powered stereo-amplifier. A red and black electric guitar leaned against the wall. The table in front of the sofa had two empty, and crushed, Bud cans, and the white ceramic ashtray was littered with old butts, about half of them smeared with lipstick.

Connie Jepson came in carrying two cans of beer. "I hope you don't mind not having a glass. Most of them are still in boxes."

"Did you move here from the ranch, Mrs. Jepson?"

"Connie, please call me Connie," she said. "No, I was living with friends. I just rented this place last week." She pushed a lock of hair from her forehead. Her face was pale, the skin clean and unblemished. She used a lot of eye shadow, and her lipstick was thick and bright red, the type the old movie stars used to wear. She was a very attractive woman, and she knew it. She sat down next to me and the couch started squeaking again.

"Have you found any of Donald's papers?" she asked.

"Papers?"

"The insurance papers. I never could find them, and I know they're somewhere there at the ranch. When can I get back there? I'd really like to find those papers and sell

81

that place." She took a dainty sip of her beer. "You do think it was murder, or an accident don't you?"

"What do you think?"

"I know it wasn't suicide. An insurance man told me they don't pay off on a suicide. And nobody in their right mind would kill themselves that way."

"I think we can rule out suicide," I said.

I was rewarded with a wide smile. I was definitely on her side.

"Mrs. Jepson, it would—"

"Please," she said, reaching over and patting my knee. "Call me Connie."

"Connie, can you think of anyone who would have wanted to kill Donald?"

"I told those other officers everything. Don was not an easy man to get along with. He made lots of enemies, at the bar, and at the ranch. He was difficult to get along with. Everything had to be his way."

"It seems a strange combination, horse trainer and bar owner."

She ran her tongue around her mouth, imparting a moist sheen to her already glossy lips.

"Don owned the place for years. I think his first wife used to run it. It was my idea to change it. I wanted to make it a first-class roadhouse, with good food and entertainment." She pointed a blood red fingernail at the guitar. "I sing, you know."

"I didn't know that."

"Yes, I'm expecting to cut an album real soon." She sucked her lips inward. "Don just didn't want to invest the money to fix the place up right."

"Did you ever hear Don mention a young man by the name of James Widmer?"

She shook her head so that the long, silky hair swished around her shoulders.

"No, I don't think so."

"How about the Alta Group, or an attorney named Sam Vickers?"

Her hair swished again.

"What about a horse named Trish's Lamb Chop?"

"Don didn't talk to me much about business, and after we were married a short time, we didn't talk about much of anything."

The telephone chirped and she went into the living room and picked it up from among the cardboard boxes. She said yes and no a half-dozen times, then, "okay, about ten minutes."

She hung up and strutted back toward me. "I'll co-operate as much as I can, Officer, and I'd really like to get back to the ranch and find those insurance papers."

I stood up. "Okay, I'll do my best to locate them for you, and if you come across anything mentioning Widmer, or the Alta Group, I'd appreciate it."

She asked for a telephone number so I gave her one where she'd get a recorded message that said, "The Hall of Justice number you've dialed is no longer in service."

I thanked her for the beer, left, started the clunker, drove it around the block, then came back and parked two houses away from Connie Jepson's place.

A few minutes later a dark blue pickup truck pulled into her driveway and the ominous figure of Leo, the bartender at The Whipcord, slid out from behind the driver's seat and trotted up the front stairs. That explained the crushed beer cans. I tried to imagine Connie Jepson and Leo as a romantic couple on my way back to my flat. It wasn't a pretty picture.

13

The morning started off badly, with an 8 AM call from Sergeant Eller.

"You were a little late with Hector Alvera's address, weren't you, Polo?"

"I saw him in the evening and advised him to contact both you and Gallegos. Then I called you the next morning. Do you want me to do all your work for you, Eller?"

"Stay out of it," Eller said, biting off the words, making each one sharp and emphatic. "I don't want some ex-cop ex-con who thinks he's a hot-shot private eye muddying up the waters, so stay out of it."

"Was Alvera any help?"

"You don't seem to listen, Polo. I don't want to see you, and I don't want to smell you, and I don't even want to hear about you sticking your nose in this case. If I want to talk to you, I'll call. You're still high up on the suspect list." He slammed the phone down so hard I had to pull the receiver away from my ear.

I called the Widmer residence, but there was no answer.

Terry Widmer wasn't listed in the phone book under *Attorneys*. I contacted the State Bar, and they showed him working at the offices of McDonald & Cullom, a big defense firm in the financial district.

Widmer was getting ready to go into a deposition. It must have been down a long hall, because he sounded out of breath when he got to the phone.

"I wonder if you could tell me the date of your brother's accident, and the name of the driver of the car?"

"Why?"

"Your brother probably had his ID on him that night."

"You were mistaken about the driver's license, Mr. Polo. I found it after you left our house. It was with Jimmy's papers that we picked up from the hospital, so I guess your theory is out the window. I'd appreciate your getting the picture I gave you back to me."

"I'll do that. But I would like to know something about that accident.

"Very well. Philip Bragga. There's been some litigation regarding the accident. We're suing the driver of the other car, Philip Bragga, but it's a case of no insurance and no assets. There's a possibility we can bring in the county for improper street design."

I thanked Terry Widmer, pushed the disconnect button on the phone, and immediately called Lieutenant Gabe Gallegos. He was available for lunch, so we set a time and place.

I stopped at the California Highway Patrol office in Redwood City and picked up a copy of the Widmer accident report. The two passengers in the Widmer car were a

Dave Church and Keith Chadway. I drove to the nearby San Mateo courthouse and checked Bragga through the civil filing indexes. There were three suits: *James Widmer vs. Bragga et al.*, *David Church vs. Bragga et al.*, and *Keith Chadway vs. Bragga et al.* Judging from my conversation with Terry Widmer, the et al. was going to turn out to be the county of San Mateo, the State of California, the city of Palo Alto, the manufacturers of the vehicles both guys were driving, the makers of the seat belts and the tires, and maybe some guy who happened to be walking his dog at the time of the accident. When the bad guy doesn't have any insurance, attorneys go on a serious litigation hunt.

Widmer had told me that Church and Chadway had received just minor injuries, but apparently some whiplashes turned up later.

I went to the file room and pulled the individual dockets. One thing of interest popped up. Keith Chadway was represented by someone from the offices of Samuel Vickers, the attorney for the Alta Group.

The relationship between a private investigator and the police is a touchy one. The private eye needs contacts in the police department. He can't work without them. Some cops, like Eller, view him as an enemy, a low life not good enough to be a real boy in blue. Some cops will ignore you their whole career, until they get ready to retire, then they will treat you like a long lost friend, because they want to get an investigator's license and find what they think will be a nice, soft, easy hobby job.

The smart cops will be cordial, push just enough information your way so that you'll cooperate and do a lot of the legwork for them. Gallegos had arranged to meet me at Pero's, a bustling restaurant a half-dozen blocks from his office. He was lounging comfortably in a red leather booth when I found him. When I sat down a waitress brought him a drink, a manhattan, up. I ordered a beer, and when the waitress left he pulled out the cherry and sucked it from its stem. There was a time when cops were more or less expected to drink on the job, but now, with Internal Affairs investigators peeping over fences and through keyholes, it was a little unusual to see one obviously enjoying a cocktail in a crowded restaurant. Gallegos seemed to be reading my mind. He chewed his cherry and took a sip of his drink. "I know where enough bodies are buried so I don't have to worry. Besides, I've got my time in." He took another sip. "Nice feeling having your time in, Polo. Things get sloppy, you just pull the plug."

"I never lasted that long."

"I know. I came close to quitting myself a few times."

The waitress came with my beer and another manhattan for Gallegos. She suggested the grilled petrale and I went along with it.

"Funny thing, you going to jail like that. Can't say I blame you too much. Must be a lot of temptation finding a half million dollars in cash."

"More temptation than I could handle." I had been working for an attorney who was trying to find his client, a drug dealer getting close to skipping out on bail. I found him, dead on a motel bed, a needle still sticking out of his arm. There was a suitcase with a half million dollars in cash lying alongside him on the bed. I can still remember just how heavy the bag felt when I picked it up. The attorney suggested we split the money. It seemed like a wonderful idea at the time. No sense in having Uncle Sam count it, store it, find out who it belonged to. We'd just keep it and save him all that trouble. It worked out fine until the attorney got cold feet and turned his money, and me, in. He got a commendation and a finder's fee, and I got a one-way ticket to Lompoc State Prison.

"Anything new on the Jepson case?" I asked.

Gallegos shook his head. "Nothing. You think they're connected? Jepson and Aiello?"

"Yes. I tried to tell Eller that, but he doesn't want to listen."

"I'm listening. Back it up."

"Aiello was killed just before he was going to make a very large bet on a horse that Jepson trained. The bet would have driven down the odds tremendously."

He went diving for the cherry in his second drink. "I know all that. Makes a good story, but there's nothing solid there. A guy like Aiello, there could be a lot of people after him. Jepson was not exactly a well-loved man himself."

"There wasn't much money bet on Jepson's horse at the track. But there was a lot of money bet at a Nevada casino, and with a local bookie."

"Your uncle?"

"No, he didn't take much of a bath. But how's this for solid. The man who collected from the local bookie, and from the casino, just happened to have died a few months before the race. And there's Jepson's wife, Connie. I visited her last night."

He tossed down his drink with a quick flip of the wrist. "Interesting visit?"

"She's terrified that somehow Jepson's death is going to be judged a suicide, and she won't get his insurance money. When I left she had a visitor. Leo, the bartender at the Whipcord."

"Leo Goens. I did some checking at the Whipcord. Leo's got the proverbial rap sheet as long as your arm. Did some time on a manslaughter charge in Los Angeles. Lot of rumors about him running drugs out of the Whipcord."

"The day I was there talking to Jepson, he was counting money in his office. Several thousand dollars in cash."

The waitress came with our fish and she and Gallegos exchanged a few pleasantries. When she was gone Gallegos pushed his fork into the sole. "Perfect," he said. "Let's eat, then talk. I think we can do business."

Over coffee I told Gallegos what I needed: a copy of the photograph on James Widmer's driver's license. I had a source in DMV who could get it for me, but it would take a couple of weeks, and a couple of hundred bucks. All Gallegos had to do was place a call to Sacramento and it would be wired to his office.

"Polo, don't you think that if someone was going to go through all the trouble of fixing a horse race, and killing Aiello and Jepson, they would be smart enough to just use a phony driver's license?"

"Sure, but it's worth a shot, Lieutenant." I handed him the photograph Terry Widmer had given me of his brother. "I showed this to the bookie who lost a lot of money on that race. It's not the man who'd been using Widmer's name, and not the man he paid off to."

Gallegos sipped his coffee slowly and said, "This bookie, is he in my neighborhood?"

"Palo Alto."

"That's close, but fortunately it's over the county line, not my jurisdiction. What's his name?"

I shook my head. We stared at each other for a while.

"Okay," Gallegos finally said. "I'll get you the DMV picture. And if it is someone other than Widmer, and your bookie friend says he's the guy he paid off, I'll want to talk to him."

The waitress cleared our plates, then handed me the check. It's a golden rule waitresses have. When two people are having lunch and one is a cop, always give the check to the other guy.

14

The police report showed that James Widmer, and the two men that were in the car with him, David Church, and Keith Chadway, all lived on Alvarado Row, Palo Alto.

It turned out to be a dorm house just off the Stanford campus. It was an older, once graceful, three-story frame house that had been chopped up to accommodate the college crowd. There was a parking lot around the side. Sitting under the shade of a half-dozen elm trees were a few BMW's, two Porsches, and a couple of Alfa-Romeo's, Mercedes, and VW convertibles. It was nice to know that the professors at Stanford weren't troubling the students with worries about the trade deficit. Good old Leland Stanford himself, when he built the university, said, "No rich man's son or daughter will want to go there. The poor alone will be welcome; it will not be built for the rich." Stanford may have been many things, but a prophet he was not.

A half-dozen old, beat-up bicycles were leaning

against the wall on the front porch. The mailbox was one of those big metal jobs, with individual boxes for letters and an open bin on the bottom for magazines and packages. There were ten boxes, and taped on each was a slip of paper with at least two or three names written in pencil, pen, or crayon. Number four showed Widmer–Chadway.

A young man in shorts carrying a tennis racket almost knocked me down as I went in the front door.

"Keith Chadway around?" I asked.

He barely paused as he rushed out the door. "No, semester ended two days ago. He's gone."

"How about Dave Church?" I asked as he pounded down the stairs.

He didn't bother to reply. I went back to the mailbox. Number seven showed Church–Fenton.

The main floor consisted of a large living room stuffed with moldy-smelling furniture. A moose head, the horns painted red and a corncob pipe stuck in its mouth, stared down sadly from over the fireplace.

Two Ping-Pong tables took up most of the dining room. The kitchen had three refrigerators. Two were full of bags labeled with names and slogans: Mike's, Jerry's, *Keep your fucking hands off*, and one that said *AIDS Virus Samples*.

The third refrigerator held nothing but beer. Corona seemed to be the brand of choice.

I walked up to the second floor. Brass numbers had been tacked to the doors. I knocked on number four. There was no response. I tried the handle; it was locked.

Room seven was up on the third floor. The door was answered by a blond girl wearing white shorts and a T-shirt that had been cut off just above her belly button.

"Is Dave Church in?" I asked.

"No, he took off."

"Do you know where I can reach him?"

She backed into the room and went over to a calendar hanging under a Gary Larson cartoon. "Let's see. He should be somewhere between Paris and Nice now."

"Paris and Nice. When's he due back?"

She shrugged her shoulders, causing the bottom of her shirt to rise up a few inches. "I don't know. A month or so. Why? Is it important?"

"I just wanted to talk to him about Jim Widmer. Did you know Jim?"

"Oh, sure. What a bummer, huh? He was a nice guy."

"Do you live here, Miss. . . ?"

"Fenton. Laura Fenton. Yeah, I've been here all semester."

"How about Keith Chadway. Do you know where I might find him?"

"Keith? He took off too. I don't know where he went. Maybe he's staying with his folks. I really don't know."

There was a small desk under the calendar littered with books, ink-stained paper cups, and the remains of a sandwich that looked like it had died from old age. "Do Keith's parents live around here?"

"Jeez, I don't know. All I know is everyone is taking off but me."

"Summer school?"

"Yeah, what a bummer, huh?"

Traffic was so bad in downtown San Francisco that I couldn't even find an open red zone or fire hydrant to park in front of. I left the car at the garage at Fifth and Mission, and walked up to Market.

Sam Vickers's office was located in the Flood Building, an old beauty built in 1904 that had survived the fire and earthquake of 1906. You can still see some of the discoloration caused by the heat of the fire in the gray colusa sandstone above the Renaissance/Baroque ornamentation above the building's main entrance.

The lobby was all marble and brass, with a high-vaulted ceiling. It made you wish that the elevator would have an operator with white gloves, but no such luck. It was the usual push-buttons and canned music.

Vickers's office was tastefully decorated. The walls were paneled in an even shade of light mahogany, the floors thickly carpeted. The receptionist was a middle-aged, middleweight, and overworked woman with a pleasant face. I introduced myself, but she had to put me on hold while she answered the phone.

"Sorry, we're so busy today, sir. Who is it you wish to see?"

"Mr. Vickers." I gave her my card.

Her smiling face dissolved into a frown. "Is he expecting you?"

"No, but if you'll just mention it's about Mr. Keith Chadway, and a murder charge, he may find the time to fit me in."

I sat in a bittersweet chocolate leather chair and flipped through copies of *Fortune* and *Forbes* while watching a a procession of men and women carrying bulging briefcases troop in and out of the office.

It took close to forty minutes, but finally the receptionist waved me over.

"He'll see you now," she said, sounding impressed.

She lead me down a narrow corridor, past doors with frosted-glass panels.

She stopped in front of a solid oak door, knocked loudly, then opened the door. I followed her into an office the size of a basketball court. Vickers was sitting behind a desk thickly covered with documents. He didn't raise his head as the receptionist handed him my card. She backpedaled softly out of the room.

Vickers was a big, heavyset man in his late fifties. He had skin the color and texture of an old saddle and a head of thick gray hair, combed straight back without a part.

He examined my business card, doing everything but biting it.

"What is this about a murder charge involving a client of mine?" he said, in a deep, modulated voice.

"I didn't say there was a murder charge involving your client. I just mentioned your client's name and the fact that there was a murder."

He pulled his head up slowly, as if it weighed a ton. "Then you gained entrance to my office under false pretenses. I'm a busy man." He waved a meaty hand toward the door. "Go."

"I tried calling you for an appointment."

"Go." Louder this time.

"I think it would be beneficial to both of us if we talked."

He expelled his breath, then reached down and picked up a yellow foolscap tablet. "Nick Polo. Private investigator, gambler, ex-con, ex-policeman. You work for a dozen or more semireputable attorneys and somehow scratch out a living, doing God knows exactly what." He dropped the tablet back on his desk. "Why would I bother talking to someone like you?"

"Stop being so sanctimonious, Vickers. You were a tough kid who came out of the Mission District, got through law school thanks to the time you served in the Army, worked hard, got lucky, worked hard, and just kept on working. But you're also a guy who likes his Scotch, and when you've had a few too many, you start calling your wife 'the plaintiff' and make eyes at anything resembling the female race."

He closed his eyes, sighed, stood up, and went over to a cabinet built into the wall, opened it, took out two glasses and a bottle of Glenlivet. He poured carefully, like a science teacher mixing solutions. He handed me a glass. It was the one with the lesser amount in it.

"Who told you about me calling my wife the plaintiff?"

"I heard you one night in Cookie's."

Cookie's had been one of the really great saloons in a town that used to be filled with them. It was located by the old Hall of Justice, and many an attorney, cop, and judge had let something slip out after one or two too many. His big face split into a smile. "Ah, Cookie's. It was a sad day when it closed down." He patted his ample stomach. "Though maybe not so sad after all." He sat back behind his desk and I dropped into what must have been "the client's chair," a comfortable black calf-covered swivel job.

"All right. Let's have it," he said.

I told him about Aiello and Jepson and the fact that the winning horse was owned by the Alta Group.

"They are clients of mine, but I don't see how that has anything to do with the other events."

"Another client of yours, Keith Chadway, was friends with a young man named James Widmer. Widmer died months ago, after being in a coma for several months. But someone has been using his ID to do some heavy gambling."

He upturned a palm. "So? You disappoint me, Mr. Polo. This has all been a waste of time. Please leave, and this time I mean it."

I finished my Scotch and put the glass down on his desk. "I think it's all connected. I'd like to talk to Chadway."

"I'd advise him against it. I repeat, sir. You are wasting my time, and my time, is expensive."

I left before he decided to charge me a consultation fee.

15

My mother had a saying. It suffers a bit in the English translation, but the basic idea is that when you are troubled, have a good meal and a good night's sleep. My father, in his wisdom, expanded it to include a bottle of red wine and a beautiful woman.

The food was no problem. I just pulled out a carton of Mrs. Damonte's homemade ravioli and some of her tomato sauce from the freezer. The wine was a Beaulieu Gamay Beaujolais, the beautiful woman was Jane Tobin. The night's sleep would come sooner or later.

I tossed a Caesar's salad and took the ravioli off the stove.

Jane inhaled the aroma from the pasta and sighed. "Ah, that smells good." She started on the salad.

"Too much garlic," she said.

"There's no such thing as too much garlic."

She sampled a ravioli.

"Ummmm, much better than that stuff in a can I've been buying."

My stomach churned at the thought of canned ravioli. The only thing that comes in a can that I trust is beer.

"What's in the filling?" Jane asked after her sixth or seventh ravioli.

The filling was a mixture of bread crumbs, Parmesan cheese, and spices, along with the main ingredient, calf's brains. I didn't think Jane would appreciate hearing that, so I told her what waiters in Italian restaurants tell their customers when asked any question they don't know the answer to. "Veal," I said.

"Delicious."

I made espresso, and after the table was cleared, Jane went to her purse and pulled out a large manila envelope. She spread the contents across the table.

"There was nothing in the paper's library on Keith Chadway. There were some articles on a Donald Chadway, who lives in Marin and won a hundred thousand in the state lottery. I didn't bother pulling those, but I thought these might be helpful." She handed me several clippings on G. K. Chadway. G. K. was a retired banker, a man who had made a fortune in the stock market, back when fortunes in the stock market were real money. He was listed as the Chief Executive Officer for several large Bay Area corporations. Most of the articles were short, eight- to ten-liners that looked like they were clipped from the paper's business section. One fairly extensive article listed his home address as Hillsborough and his hobby as horse breeding. Bingo. Just the kind of a chap to be a client of Sam Vickers.

I had asked Jane to check on David Church, Leo

Goens, and James and Terry Widmer. "Nothing on any of the others," she said.

"Pretty lady, you done good as they say in certain parts of town. You've earned dessert. Anything you want. If I don't have it, and can't make it, I'll run out and buy it."

"Something without garlic," she said.

I was down at Lieutenant Gallegos's office by ten the next morning. He wasn't in, but his secretary handed me an envelope with my name scrawled on it.

The DMV photostat of James Widmer's driver's license showed the picture of a young man with bushy dark hair, a big mustache, and horn-rimmed glasses with lenses the size of hubcaps. It certainly looked nothing like the picture Terry Widmer had given me of his brother.

The license showed that it had been reissued just three months ago, at a time when poor James was in a coma. It made sense. Show up at the Department of Motor Vehicles office. Tell them you lost your wallet and your license. They take your word for it. Take another photo, and send it to the address on the license. Much easier than going through the trouble of buying or making a forged license. The only hitch was you had to have access to the mailbox where the license was sent to. In Widmer's case it was the Stanford dormitory on Alvarado Row.

G. K. Chadway wasn't listed in the telephone book, and since Hillsborough was in San Mateo County, all I had to do to check voters registration files was take the elevator from Gallegos's office down to the main floor of the Hall of Records building.

Chadway was registered to vote at 1145 Finchwood Way. The assessor's office was a block away. They showed G. K. Chadway as the resident of the Finchwood address, as well as owner of several acres on Whiskey Hill Road in Woodside. The map book showed the Woodside property bordered parts of Dallera Road, right near Jepson's ranch. Now, wasn't that interesting?

I tried the Hillsborough address first. It was a big, rambling Tudor place, hidden from the wooded road by a head-high brick fence. Topiary hedges were scattered around a flawless lawn. There was a long pool dotted with lily ponds leading to the front of the house. The door was answered by a young woman in a maid's uniform. She had an Irish accent.

"Mr. Chadway is gone, sir."

"Do you know when he'll be back?"

"Not until September."

"What about Keith?"

Her dimples seemed to flatten out a bit at the mention of Keith.

"He's not at home now, sir, and I don't know when he's expected. Can I leave him a message?"

"Yes, thank you." I handed her one of my cards.

"When did you last see Keith?"

"He's in and out quite often, sir." She gave me one last look at those dimples, then closed the door softly.

I went back to the car, got out my Thomas Guide map book, and pointed the car's nose to Woodside.

Chadway's place had a brick entrance fence with wagon wheels embedded in it. A metal sign with the initials GKC hung over the gated entrance. The road was straight and dusty and was bordered by a neatly groomed hedge of alternating red and white oleanders. It led to a complex of adobe buildings with real red-tile roofs and the obligatory barn and stables. As I parked the car a young

101

Latin, still in his early teens, ran over and opened the door for me.

"Yes, sir," he said enthusiastically. "Can I help you?" He was wearing clean denim pants, a spotless white shirt, and a red bandana around his neck that looked like it was just out of the box.

"I'm looking for Keith Chadway," I said.

He looked my car over with eyes older than the rest of him. "Is there a problem, sir?"

"No, none at all. Is he around?"

"Yes, I will escort you."

I followed his lead past the adobe buildings, around to the stables. There were horses everywhere, being walked, being ridden, being brushed down.

"Busy place," I said to my escort.

"Oh, yes. Always busy, sir. Are you in the market for a horse?"

"Not yet. Does Chadway train his own horses?"

"Oh, yes. The pleasure horses, and the breeding horses, but not the racehorses. He takes . . ."

Someone yelled out, "Pedro, get over here," and the boy broke off in midsentence. He swiveled his neck, smiled at me, and said, "Mr. Chadway is over by breeding stall number seventeen, sir. Excuse me."

He took off at a full trot toward two men dressed in working cowboy outfits.

The stalls were all numbered in heavy black paint. There was a group of four men and two women standing in front of number seventeen. They were busy chatting away and didn't notice me until I was right up next to them.

"Keith Chadway?" I asked.

Three of the men were in their thirties, the women

slightly younger. They were all dressed in designer jeans and expensive-looking shirts and suede coats. The women had knuckle-to-knuckle diamonds.

The youngest of the group, no more than twenty-four, turned toward me. "I'm Chadway," he said. He was good sized: six one or two, and had on a pair of beige cords, held up by a belt with an enormous silver buckle. His hair was a dirty blond and was starting to thin at the temples. In another ten years there wouldn't be much left. His eyes were covered by a pair of mirrored sunglasses. There was a large bandage on his left forearm.

"Can I talk to you a moment, Mr. Chadway?"

"I'm busy," he said, turning his back on me. He put his arms around one of the women. "Come on inside. For this kind of money, you might as well get a good look."

Everyone laughed and followed him into the stall. There was a whitewashed fence of heavy wood planking. Behind the fence was a horse, the head in some type of a harness, tied to a fence that was padded with carpeting. The horse had what looked to be rubber boots over its hind feet. Its tail was wrapped with thick white adhesive tape.

Pedro, the same young man who had met me at my car, led another horse into the stall. Two cowboys came over and took the horse's reins from him.

Keith Chadway climbed over the fence separating him from the horses and grabbed the reins of the horse that had been led in. The horse's eyes were bulging as he was led over to the other horse. They nuzzled their noses together and made horse noises for a few moments, then Chadway yelled, "They're ready. I'll lead the stud."

One of the women said, "Just like a male, minimal foreplay." They all laughed.

Chadway grabbed the stud's reins and carefully led him directly behind the mare tied to the fence.

Pedro hopped over the fence and walked outside. I decided to join him.

He was lighting a cigarette and leaning against the side of a stall when I caught up to him.

"I thought they did all their breeding by artificial insemination now," I said.

He spoke jerkily between puffs on the cigarette.

"Just for certain horses, sir. Palominos, pintos, Appaloosas, quarter horses, but not for Arabians, hackneys, or Thoroughbreds."

"Why don't they just let them out in the pasture and let nature take its course?"

He laughed. "Too much chance of one of the horses getting injured. That's why we put the kicking boots on the mare. She kick a stallion in the wrong place with one of those hoofs, and she could cause a lot of damage."

"Is there a lot of money in horse breeding?"

He shook his hand like it was burning. "Much, much money, sir."

"How did Chadway hurt his arm?"

He dropped his butt to the dirt and ground it out under his heel. "I really don't know, sir. I better get back."

I waited close to fifteen minutes. Chadway and his friends came out of the stall. The men were laughing. The women looked a little flushed in the face.

They shook hands all around and Chadway headed back to the stall.

I called out to him. "Chadway, got a minute?"

He stopped and looked at his watch. "Not much more."

"I spoke to Sam Vickers yesterday."

He slid his sunglasses down to the end of his nose and looked at me with pallid blue eyes.

"What about?"

"Jim Widmer."

He pushed his glasses back up. Wrinkles of annoyance spread across his forehead. "You're that Polo guy."

"That's right. I just wanted to ask you a few questions about—"

"Look out for that horse behind you," he shouted.

I pivoted around, then felt a blow on the back of my neck. I dropped to the ground and tried to get up. A boot caught me in the stomach, and as I doubled over I felt another blow to my neck.

I came to sitting in my car. Pedro was leaning in the window.

"Are you feeling all right now, sir?"

I rubbed my neck. "No. Where's Chadway?"

"He left, sir. He said you walked right into one of the horses. Should I call a doctor, sir?"

I was getting a little tired of all the sirs. "Look, Pedro. It wasn't a horse I ran into. Didn't you see what happened?"

He stood back from the car and raised both hands in the air. "No one saw anything but Mr. Chadway, sir."

"Give him a message for me Pedro. Tell him this town isn't big enough for both of us, and I'll meet him in front of the Long Branch at sunup."

He just stared at me. I guess he was too young to have been brought up on westerns. I should have said something about meeting Chadway in the next galaxy and to make sure he brought his laser gun.

I turned over the motor and rode out toward the sunset.

16

Since it was only a couple of miles away, I drove by Jepson's ranch. The gate was closed. A big, new-looking chrome padlock was clipped around the gate's latch. It would have been a simple matter, even in my condition, to climb over the fence, but there didn't seem to be much point in it.

I massaged my neck with one hand while I drove down the freeway to Sand Hill Road, then east to Stanford University. I wedged my car in between two VW convertibles parked on Alvarado. A serious-looking young woman was sitting on the front steps reading a paperback novel. I tilted my head trying to see the title, but she closed the book and folded it under her arms.

"Can I help you?" she said.

"I wanted to see Laura Fenton, Dave Church's roommate."

"She's not in."

"How about Keith Chadway?"

"He's not in either."

I sat down beside her. She had thick eyebrows and what looked like a permanent scowl pressed into her face.

"Maybe you can help me," I said, pulling out the DMV photograph. "Do you recognize this man?"

She flicked her eyes at the picture, then said, "Are you a cop?"

"No, I'm—"

"Then how come you're driving a cop car?"

"I bought it used. It was all I could afford. I'm a private investigator looking for a missing young man. He left a young girl. He didn't know he had gotten her pregnant. She had twins. The man's a father now and doesn't even know it." I pushed the picture back at her.

She didn't even bother to look at it. "You're really full of shit, mister. I know a narc when I see one." She stood up and went inside, slamming the door after her.

I started toward the car, then turned around and headed toward the campus. Bobby North told me he had made all his payments and pickups at something called Tresidder Union.

I flagged down a Chinese kid on a bicycle and he pointed me in the right direction.

Tresidder Memorial Union turned out to be a large outdoor patio. There were something like seventy white metal tables surrounded by white metal mesh chairs, set under a few oak trees. There were circles of blooming impatiens in neat flower boxes, ten newspaper vending machines offering everything from the student newspaper to the *Wall Street Journal*, a black granite Benny Bufano statue of a faceless man and woman hugging a rock, and metal parking racks filled with the omnipresent bicycles.

107

All in all, a pleasant place to stop for lunch, to study, to meditate, or to buy drugs and pick up the winnings from a bookie like Bobby North. There was a university version of a 7-Eleven store, simply called the Store, selling sandwiches, soft drinks, and coffee. I bought a cup of coffee and wandered around.

I tried showing the DMV picture to a few of the kids sitting at the tables, but all I got were dumb looks, head shakes, and more scowls.

I went back to the car and headed down to Bobby North's place. It was only about a ten-minute drive, but the real estate value dropped about twenty thousand a minute as I drove into the industrial area of East Palo Alto.

I pounded on North's door for a minute or two. Nothing. I walked around the back. There were dozens of old tires and car parts leaning against the adjoining building. I dragged two tires over and stood on top of them and peered into North's back window. The glass had been sprayed with white paint. I used a key to scrape enough off to give me a view of the inside. The same desks and phones and tape recorders I'd seen on my last visit. But no people. Bookies are like prostitutes; they never have a day when there aren't willing customers. I could hear the phones ringing. North was passing up a lot of bets by not having his people manning the phones.

I drove back to San Francisco. Mrs. Damonte was hosing down the front again, and she grudgingly moved the hose as I put the car in the garage.

"Everything okay, Mrs. Damonte?" I said cheerfully.

"Nopa."

108

She was back to English, which indicated a bad mood. Maybe nobody had died and she had no wake to go to. I showered, keeping the hot water pounding on the sore spot on the back of my neck, made myself a quick tuna sandwich, then walked three blocks to Uncle Pee Wee's place.

He was back in his office.

"Any good news?" he asked.

"I'm not sure." I handed him the DMV picture. "I'd like to show this to the people at the Fiesta in Reno. See if this is the man they paid off."

He studied the picture. "Talk to John Boscacci. I'll tell him to expect you. It matches the description they gave me: big mustache, glasses." He raised his eyes to mine. "Who is he?"

"That's the picture on James Widmer's driver's license. But it's not Widmer. This picture was taken after Widmer was injured and in a coma."

"Then who is it, Nicky?"

"That's what I'm working on, Uncle. I stopped by Bobby North's place a little while ago. I wanted to show the picture to him. His place was empty."

He brought his hands together in a loud clap. "North. He called me after you saw him. Made threats. He's a fool. You're sure his place is empty?"

"I looked in the back. No one there. The phones were ringing off the hook."

He leaned forward with his elbows on the desk. "That's not good, Nicky. There is no way that he should not be on line, right now. The man is foolish enough to work out of one shop. That's crazy. Nowadays you must have phone relays. The safe way is to use two or three relays, so you're always a good distance from the actual incoming phone. With today's electronics, you could run your shop here in San Francisco from Naples. But North is too lazy. The money is too easy for him. He can't last."

He wiped the back of his hand across his mouth, as if wiping away a bad taste. "If he's not open today, then he's in serious trouble. The police have him or he's dead."

I was expecting a message on my answering machine from either Sergeant Eller, Lieutenant Gallegos, or some other unknown cop saying that North had been found dead and I was the number one suspect, but the only message was from Jane Tobin. It was short and to the point. "I'm hungry."

I called her at work. "Dinner?" I asked.

"Where?"

"It'll be a surprise. See if you can find someone at the paper who knows some bars where the kids from Stanford hang out. And dress casual. Put on one of your teenybopper outfits. I'd like you to look very young, very student bodyish."

"My, my, you are getting kinky."

"Just how do you describe kinky, lady?"

"If you have to ask, you're not flexible enough. Pick me up at six."

She was wearing tight denim pants that were so faded they were almost white, and a forest green blouse that tied at the back of the neck, leaving her back completely bare, and making it obvious that there was no possible way she could be wearing a bra. Her hair was brushed back and tied in a ponytail. She had on a pair of those goofy-looking black leather basketball shoes. She looked about seventeen.

She put a hand on her hip. "Well?"

"I'm afraid," I said.

"Afraid of what?"

"Afraid I'll get accused of statutory rape."

She patted my cheek, a little harder than necessary. "I'll take that as a compliment."

I drove back down to Palo Alto. We started at the "Big O," as it has been known on the Stanford campus for twenty years. It was a big, rowdy joint, famous for its huge hamburgers and oversized mugs of beer. The parking lot was jammed, so we had to park a good block away. The night was warm on the peninsula, so Jane left her jacket in the car.

"Okay, go over it again," she said.

I handed her the DMV picture. "You're going to show this around, tell them his name is Jim and you're trying to find him, met him at a party, never got his last name."

She took the picture and looked at it closely. "And Jim was supposed to give me this picture? It looks like a mug shot."

"If they ask, just tell them you had it cropped from another picture that the two of you were in, or a group picture, whatever. You met the guy, you've got the hots for him."

She looked at the picture again. "He looks like a would-be terrorist. Why don't *you* flash the damn picture?"

"Because all of these upstanding youngsters, the cream of one of America's finest universities, the future of this great country of ours, will think I'm a narc and beat the hell out of me. Just try to make sure they look at the picture and not at your boobs. You know you can see them when you lean a certain way in that blouse?"

She smiled brightly. "That's why they make the blouses like that, stupid."

The "Big O" was located on the bottom floor of an old frame building. The walls were dark, covered by posters and cooking grease. The tables were wood, the tops layered with dozens of coats of varnish that had initials, political slogans, and sexual advice scratched into them. An open kitchen was throwing out smoke from the hamburger grill.

"Are we eating here?" Jane asked.

"This is a drink-here-but-don't-eat-here kind of place." We went to the bar; Jane ordered a white wine and I asked for a beer. When the bartender delivered our drinks, Jane pulled out the picture and went into her act. I faded away. Most of the tables were jammed with young college kids. Outside of the bartender, I figured I had to be the oldest guy in the place.

There were a few pinball and video games against one wall. I started feeding quarters into one of them, while keeping my eye on Jane. She had moved from the bar and was over by the kitchen. Smart girl. Talk to the help first. She made her way to the tables, staying a few minutes at each, passing the picture around. One tall, muscular kid in his twenties, with linebacker shoulders, had his arm around Jane's back. His hand started edging up her back and around to the side of her blouse. He was hunched over her, laughing. Suddenly he straightened up as if he'd stepped on a hot plate. Then he reached down and started massaging his ankle.

Jane came over shaking her head.

"Get me out of here, Polo. The natives are starting to get restless."

"You seemed to take the starch out of Tarzan's loincloth. Are you okay?"

"Oh, sure. But we're not doing much good. No one recognized the picture, but if you want to go to a party later tonight, I've had seven offers so far."

"I doubt if I'm included in the invitation. Let's try again down the road."

We went a few blocks north to the British Banker's Club, a stone building that was actually once a bank and had been converted into a yuppie bar-restaurant. The place was jammed. The crowd a little older than at the Big O. Instead of Levi's and sweatshirts, the men had cords and tweed coats. The women were wearing the kind of casual stuff they only sell at Saks and Neiman-Marcus.

I followed Jane around for a few minutes. It was a pleasure to walk behind her for more than the obvious reasons. She would have made a chiropractor a fortune the way she was making the boys twist their necks. I sat at the bar. The kid next to me ordered a drink. The bartender poured a little crushed ice into an old-fashioned glass, put in a shot of tequila, topped it off with some club soda, then picked up the glass, put a towel over the top, and suddenly slammed it down on the top of the bar. The customer picked it up and gulped it down while it was still foaming.

"What's that called?" I asked the bartender.

"A popper. Want to try one?"

"Sure."

One turned out to be enough. If for some reason you wanted to get blind, stinking drunk in a hurry, that was the way to go, I guess. The kid next to me was on his third popper when I saw Laura Fenton. She was at a table with another girl and two guys who looked like they modeled swim suits: blond hair, perfect tans, muscles showing under rolled-up shirt sleeves. Jane was heading in their direction. I watched as she went into her act. The picture got passed around the table, and while the two sun gods turned their smiles on Jane, Laura Fenton pushed the picture back and forth in front of her face like she was playing a trombone. She laughed, then handed it back to Jane.

I waved her over to the bar. "You're earned a drink. If the bartender doesn't ask you for an ID, I'm buying."

She gave me the kind of smile you get from an Internal Revenue auditor when you tell him you've lost your receipts for that particular deduction.

"My, my. What a big spender."

She ordered a white wine.

"That table you were just at, Jane. What happened?"

"Nothing, really. This doesn't seem to be going anywhere, Nick. And I'm getting very hungry."

"That one girl looked like she might have known something."

Jane took a sip of her drink. "I think she needs glasses. Besides, they were all pretty high."

I looked back toward the table Laura Fenton was sitting at. A waiter came over and handed out menus.

"Time to get out of here," I said.

"Already? Gee, this was turning out to be such a

swell date. What next, Polo? To the creamery for a malt? Then maybe we can sit on the swing on my front porch. But no hand-holding. Daddy may be watching."

"No. Something even more fun than that."

"A panty raid?"

"In a way, yes."

17

"Just what the hell do you plan to do with that?" Jane Tobin asked, as I reached over her lap, opened the glove compartment, and took out a Swiss Army knife.

"Don't ask. Just do me a favor. Wait here, and if any kids come by and start up the stairs, beep the horn, okay?"

"No, not okay. I don't mind helping you out, lover, but I've got a certain interest here. A story. And sitting alone in this jalopy on a dark street just doesn't cut it. I mean, I don't mind playing Nora to your Nick Charles, but this is pushing it. Besides, I'm starving."

"Lobster, steak, veal. Anything you want. Just give me a few minutes."

She peered out the car window. "What the hell is in that old house, anyway?"

"James Widmer used to live there."

"And you're going to do what? Break into his room?"

I held up a protesting hand. "That would be attempted burglary. A felony. A man, or woman, could go to jail for that. So, please, just sit in the car for a few minutes, then I promise, the rest of the night we'll do whatever you want."

She chuckled. She had a great dirty chuckle. "Anything I want? I don't think you'd have the stamina. I may end up going to one of those parties I was invited to."

I kissed her lightly on the lips, then got out of the car. The front door was unlocked, the lights were on in the living room. The moose head looked even sadder than the last time I'd seen it.

There was no one in sight. Why the hell would a college kid be home on a Friday night, anyway? I made my way up to the second floor, and knocked lightly on the door to room number four, the room Widmer had been sharing with Keith Chadway. I counted to thirty, knocked again, then took out the Swiss Army knife. It was the deluxe model, the one with everything but a hatchet and a pair of binoculars on it. It's not the best tool in the world for picking locks, in fact it's no good at all, unless you make some alterations to the fish scaler, but it has one advantage that those nicely tooled lock picks don't have: If the cops catch you with it, all it looks like is a Swiss Army knife.

I used the altered fish scaler and the tweezers, and after raking away for less than a minute heard that satisfying click as the lock turned.

I went in quickly and turned on the light. There were two small bedrooms, one empty, nothing but a bed frame and box springs. The closet held a few shirts and sport coats. The coats looked expensive. I checked for a label. There were none, but the name Keith Chadway

117

was stitched in red letters on the lining. There was a small dresser. The drawers were all empty.

The other room had a bed with a brown corduroy cover. The closet held more sport clothes and a charcoal gray suit, again with Chadway's name stitched on the lining. A half-dozen pairs of shoes, ranging from sneakers to snakeskin cowboy boots, were neatly spaced on the closet's floor.

The dresser, a duplicate of the one in the other room, held an array of folded shorts, T-shirts, and socks.

The kitchen–sitting room was nothing special. It had a small hot plate, an old refrigerator. I opened up the fridge. Nothing but beer, Rose's lime juice, cocktail onions, and olives. The small freezer was crammed with an ice tray and a half-filled bottle of Stolichnaya vodka.

I checked through the kitchen drawers; nothing there that shouldn't have been there.

I tried the bathroom next. The medicine chest held a few over-the-counter cold drugs, shaving cream, and a package of disposable razors. A styptic pencil was encased in its clear, round container. There were blood stains on the end of the pencil. I put it in my pocket, then went back to the bedroom and got on my knees and looked under the bed. Nothing. Not even a dust ball. One thing you had to say for Chadway. He was neat. A no-good bastard, but neat.

I ran my hand under the mattress and felt something slick. I pulled it out. A magazine entitled *Boys Will Be Boys*. There were pictures of young men, very young men, engaged in acts of, as they say in the police reports, "oral copulation and sodomy." Only this magazine was a little more explicit, with pictures titled things like, "Little Sucker," and "Cheek-to-Cheek Party."

I pulled the mattress up. There were a half-dozen or more magazines, all catering to the same thing: men fondling baby-faced kids. I threw the magazine back and dropped the mattress, then went to the bathroom and washed my hands.

I got out of there and made my way up to room number seven on the third floor. Practice must make perfect, because it took me only a few seconds to spring the lock on the door to the Laura Fenton–Dave Church apartment. I was just about to enter when I heard someone come in the front door.

I waited, peeking over the banister, until I saw Jane walking slowly up the stairs. She saw me and said, "Your five minutes are up, buster."

"I thought one of the greatest attributes a reporter could have was patience."

"I've run out. Feed me or give me something to write about," she said, as she came up alongside me and peered into the open door.

"Did you hear that?" I said.

"What?"

"Sounds like someone is calling for help."

She looked me square in the eye. "I don't hear anything."

"Well, in case the cops ask, remember I said I did when I found this open door." I pushed the door all the way open with my foot, went in, felt for the light switch, and clicked it on. Nothing much seemed to have changed since my last visit, though at least the sandwich was no longer rotting away on the desk.

It was the same layout as the Chadway–Widmer apartment; two small bedrooms and the kitchen–sitting room. The first bedroom was Laura's. The bed was unmade; pink sheets with yellow and red flowers spilled over a pink blanket. Colorful underwear—panties, bras, stockings—cascaded out of open drawers. The walls were decorated with posters of animals: cats hanging from trees, kittens stuffed into socks, puppies sleeping under a Christmas tree.

The adjoining room had a few posters too: young gorgeous girls in string bikinis. The bed was stripped. The bureau drawers held a few of the bare essentials and the closet had a lone pair of shoes, two shirts, and a pair of gray slacks hanging from a nail. There was a box stuffed with newspapers lying next to the shoes. I dragged it out and lifted out a few of the papers. Racing forms. I dug through the box. The forms went back for several months. There were all kinds of unreadable scribbled notes on almost every page. Horses' names were circled in red or scratched out. Numbers, probably the final odds, were also in red alongside the various listed horses.

"Find anyone needing help?" Jane said.

"Just me." I riffed through the racing forms. There were none for the date Johnny Aiello was killed at the track.

I pushed the box back into the closet, then ran my fingers through the pockets of the gray slacks. I came up with a quarter, a dime, and a cheap ball-point pen. The pen had a motel's name printed on it. The Sundial, Reno, Nevada. I slipped it in my pocket.

There was a small end table next to the bed. The top drawer held a large jar of Vaseline, a packet of Kleenex, and some cough drops.

The bottom drawer had a stack of magazines—*Penthouse, Playboy, Hustler*—and a white vinyl photo album. I flipped through the pictures. There were several of a tall, curly-haired kid in his late teens with his arms around a middle-aged man and woman. There was a noticeable resemblance between the boy and the man. There were pictures of the same boy, a few years older now, sitting around a swimming pool with a group of kids of similar age. I recognized one of the girls as Laura Fenton. Another picture had Laura with her arms around him. It was signed, "To Dave, the world's cheapest roommate, Laura."

Finally, there was a group of six pictures, the kind you take in one of those little curtained booths at the beach or game arcades. Dave Church was making faces at the camera while a pretty girl with a mass of long red hair sat on his lap. In the last picture he was alone, and smiling almost normally at the camera.

Jane was tapping her foot. "I'm still hungry, Nick."

"Turn your back a second."

When she turned around, I tore out that last photograph of Church.

We went back to the British Banker's Club. Laura Fenton and her friends had already gone. We both had the catch of the day, which actually tasted like it was caught that day; sea bass done in a light tomato sauce.

"That was delicious," Jane said, digging into the last bite of her cheesecake.

"How can you eat like that and stay so slim and beautiful?"

"My boyfriend's a second-story man. I get to hold the ladder for him next time."

"Must be exciting."

She dropped her fork to the plate with a clunk. "Did you really find out anything tonight?"

I handed her Dave Church's picture. "Put a mustache, a wig and a pair of glasses on this guy, then compare it to the DMV photograph. Could it be the same guy?"

Jane held the two pictures up and studied them, tilting her head from one side to the other. "Could be, Nick, but honestly, there's no way to say for sure." She looked around the restaurant. "Probably half the kids in here could be made up to look like this guy," she said, tapping her fingernail against the DMV photo.

"Yes, I'm afraid you're right."

"Does that mean all this supersleuthing we've done tonight was for naught?"

"Well, Nora, we didn't exactly crack the case. And you know what Mr. and Mrs. Charles always did when things were troubling them, don't you?"

She covered her face with her hands, peeking at me through the fingers. "I'm afraid to ask."

"Had a drink and went to bed."

18

The Federal Bureau of Investigation did a study, and after exhaustive research and oodles of taxpayers' money, concluded that a human being sleeps the soundest between 3:30 AM and 4:30 AM. So, if you are going to bust down a door and find the bad guys dozing off, that's the best time to do it. There must be a lot of truth in it, because when the phone rang, I didn't even hear it.

Jane elbowed me in the ribs several times. "Answer the goddamned phone," she said, in a less than cheerful manner.

"Sherwood Forest, Robin Hood speaking," I mumbled into the receiver. Let's face it, who the hell can come up with a real good line when the digital alarm clock is showing 4:18 AM?

"Polo. You know a guy named Robert Collin North?"

It took me a second to recognize Inspector Tehaney's dulcet tones.

"Could be."

"Well, he's got your business card in his wallet. At least what's left of your card—it's pretty much a mass of pulp right now. But then so is North. You know where Fort Point Lifeboat Station is?"

"In the Presidio," I answered, ending the sentence with a loud yawn.

"Right. Come on down. Now."

Jane was half-awake, lying back on her elbows, the sheet down far enough to expose her breasts. It was a lovely sight.

"What's that all about?"

"A cop. Wants me to come and meet him at the Coast Guard Station in the Presidio. I think it's another dead body."

"Whose?"

"Bobby North. A bookie."

She pulled back the sheets and started to get up.

"If I bring you, the cop won't talk to me."

She flopped back down on the mattress. "Are you just trying to talk me out of coming?"

I patted her bare shoulder. "That's something I'd never try to talk you out of, darling."

She stuck her tongue out at me and pulled the covers up over her head. "I expect a detailed report when you get back," she said in a muffled voice.

The Presidio was originally founded all the way back in 1776, by some Spaniard who had come up from Mexico, plotting out military bases and missions. The army takes up about ninety-nine percent of the place. It's the Sixth U.S. Army headquarters; there are several reserve units, an excellent hospital, Old Fort Point, an actual fort with

124

massive forty-foot-thick walls, and cannon batteries. Located at the foot of the Golden Gate Bridge, it was built in the early 1860s, during the Civil War, to protect the harbor in case of an attack, which never came. You'll remember it from Hitchcock's classic, *Vertigo*, where Kim Novak jumped in the bay and James Stewart dove in after her. There's a national cemetery, a historic museum, an officer's club (which is the second oldest building in San Francisco, the oldest being Mission Dolores), enlisted men's clubs, barracks, officers' residences, a post office, a theater, and a small airport, all situated on fifteen hundred of the most beautiful, tree-filled acres in San Francisco. Real estate developers weep and break out in hives when they drive by.

The one percent of the Presidio that the army doesn't control is occupied by Fort Point Lifeboat Station, a beautiful cluster of old Victorian buildings painted white, with red peaked-shingle roofs.

I parked under a palm tree next to an ambulance. The lights were on inside the biggest of the buildings. A dock led out to a boat house. There were a half-dozen or so people standing around at the end of the dock. The flooring creaked under my weight as I made my way to the crowd. The fog had come into the bay, almost obscuring the Golden Gate Bridge. Two white Coast Guard cutters bobbed up and down, bumping against the padded pier, their mooring lines making lifelike groaning sounds. Fog horns were moaning in the distance, and a wind cold enough to remind you it was summer in San Francisco came off the choppy water and made me glad that I had worn a turtleneck sweater under my jacket.

Members of the ambulance crew, a heavyset man in his forties with hair too dark to go with the rest of his

125

body, and a tall, thin woman with a knit cap pulled over her head, was bending over a tubular metal body-basket.

Three Coast Guardsmen, none older than twenty-five, wearing denim pants, heavy parkas, and blue base-ball-style caps, were leaning against the boat house trying to look bored. Who knows? Maybe they weren't trying. Maybe pulling stiffs out of the water becomes routine.

There was a string of stick-man figures stenciled on the side of the boat house, showing the number of bodies the crew had pulled from the bay since January. The man in the basket was going to be number seventeen.

Tehaney was puffing away on a cigarette, his thin sandy hair blowing across his face.

"Take a look, Polo. See if it's North."

The ambulance crew moved out of the way. It was Bobby North all right. His face was blue and bloated and something had been nibbling at his skin, but it was North.

Tehaney must have been reading my mind. "Makes you want to give up Crab Louis, doesn't it? Is it him?"

"Yeah."

He turned his attention to one of the sailors. "And you're sure he was in San Francisco waters, huh? Couldn't have been in San Mateo?"

"I told you, Inspector, he was floating out by Hunter's Point. San Mateo County doesn't come into play until you're past Candlestick Park."

Tehaney flicked his cigarette into the bay. "Okay, boys and girls. He's ours. Take him away."

The ambulance crew transferred North's body from the rescue basket to a gurney and started wheeling him back toward the parking lot. We followed a few feet be-hind.

"Damn body floated south another mile or so and it would be San Mateo's problem."

"Any idea where he actually died?"

"No. You never can tell, the tides bump them around like hockey pucks. Guy jumps off the bridge, he could wind up being found over in Oakland, or fifteen or twenty miles out to sea. Or not found at all."

We watched as the gurney was put into the back of the ambulance.

"The coroner should get more money," Tehaney said. "Imagine making your living by cutting up something like that. Come on, let's get some coffee."

He led me into the base kitchen, a high-ceilinged room with lifesavers from old ships on the wall. There was a restaurant-sized coffee urn on the sink. Tehaney poured coffee into two thick white mugs and we sat at a long table covered with a red plastic tablecloth.

"Tell me about this North guy," Tehaney said, blowing on his coffee to cool it down.

I told him everything I knew about North, leaving out only my rather embarrassing encounter with Keith Chadway, and the fact that I had broken into two apartments on the Stanford campus the night before.

He took a plastic bag from his overcoat pocket and dumped it on the table. "This is all North had on him." He opened the bag and shook out the contents. There was a wallet, a gold money clip in the shape of a horse's head holding a few twenties, a leather key holder that held six keys, a handkerchief, and a gold Blancpain watch.

Tehaney opened up the wallet. "Your card was behind his driver's license, in this plastic holder. That's what kept it from turning to mush."

"I told Lieutenant Gallegos that I'd keep him posted on what was going on. He's going to be interested to hear about North."

"Where was North running his bookie operation?"

"East Palo Alto." I gave him the address and he wrote it in his notebook.

"You talked to North down there? And he was taking book at the time?"

"I heard phones ringing. I don't think he was running an answering service."

Tehaney sighed and scraped the wallet and everything else back into the plastic bag. "Two bookies dead in a matter of a few days, Nick."

"Johnny Aiello got killed just before he was trying to knock down the odds on a certain horse. North was the lone bookie in the Bay Area to take a heavy hit on that race. And Don Jepson, the horse's trainer, gets kicked to death."

Tehaney groaned and scratched his head. "I'm going to have to get together with Gallegos and Eller on this."

"Gallegos got me a DMV picture from James Widmer's license." I handed it across the table to Tehaney. "I'm going to have it checked by the people in Reno who lost money on that race."

He flicked the picture with his thumb. "This the only copy you've got?"

"Yep."

He handed it back to me. "I'll get a few more. I'm going to have to talk to your uncle, too. And that bartender guy, what the hell was his name?"

"Goens. Leo Goens. He's at the Whipcord during

the day, but I wouldn't try to talk to him there. Not unless you bring a few members of the tactical squad with you. He's chummy with Jepson's widow. She lives out on South Mayfair in Daly City.

Tehaney stripped the cellophane wrapper off a new pack of Lucky's and lit up. He looked at me through a plume of smoke. "Whatever you know and you're not telling me, I hope it doesn't come out later and bite you in the ass, Nick."

"You think I'm holding something back?"

He shrugged. "Sure. People always hold things back in a case like this. You're involved personally because of your uncle. I understand that. If you want to jack off Gallegos and Eller, it's no sweat to me." His soft gray eyes hardened. "But this North character is my case now. I'm stuck with it. You get something, you tell me." He dropped his cigarette into the remains of his coffee, then stood up and stretched. "I'll let you know what the coroner comes up with," he said, as he shuffled out to his car.

Mrs. Damonte caught me coming up the stairs. Even though it was only seven in the morning, she was dressed in full battle gear: black dress, sturdy shoes, hair neatly done up in a bun. She invited me inside by waving a finger at me.

Her place was a strange mixture of scents: garlic, spices, furniture polish, and Lysol. Everything was always spotless. I followed her into the kitchen, which was giving off delicious baking smells.

"That girl, you going to marry her?" she said.

"Nopa."

She nodded her head and smiled briefly. Her master plan was for me to end up marrying one of her seemingly endless supply of young nieces and cousins that came over from Italy every few months. Marry, then move down the peninsula, or across the bay to Marin County in a nice ranch-style home, leaving her in full charge of the flats.

She handed me a tray of cannoli, crisp tubes of pastry dough filled with cream and candied cherries.

"Give some to the skinny one," she said, then rapped her fingers against a kitchen cabinet. "Needs paint."

I had just painted the whole damn kitchen myself two years ago, using the glossiest, toughest enamel I could find. The cabinets had been as white and bright as the side of a new ocean liner. Now they were dull and chalky, the result of daily scouring. I wished she'd use all that energy for something else. Like moving furniture. Hers.

I thanked her for the cannoli and let myself into my flat. Jane was still in bed. I got the coffee going, and when it was made, put a pot, two cups, and several of the cannoli on a tray and brought it into the bedroom.

"Rise and shine, lady. Checkout time is noon."

Jane pulled her head from under the covers. "What smells so damn good?"

"Mrs. D. made us breakfast."

"The little old lady downstairs? How did she know I was here? We came in awfully late."

"She never sleeps. Constantly on guard." I passed her one of the pastries. "Here, try one."

She took a bite and moaned with pleasure. "Ummmmm, these could make you fat real quick. Tell me, what happened?"

I gave her a brief synopsis of my meeting with Tehaney.

"What are you going to do now?" she said.

130

I started undressing. "Catch up on that sleep I lost. Thanks for keeping the bed warm," I said, slipping in next to her.

She picked another cannoli off the tray, took a bite, then let some of the cream spill out onto my chest.

"My, my, I made a mess," she said, then dropped down and started licking off the whipped cream.

"That's what I love about you, Jane. You're so neat."

19

By the time I dropped Jane off at her apartment, it was close to eleven. I stopped at a photography lab on 2nd Street and arranged to have copies made of the DMV photograph of whoever the hell was on James Widmer's license, and copies of the picture of Dave Church that I'd swiped from his room at Stanford. Since I wanted them right away, I had to settle for macro-photos of the ones I had. Those I could pick up in an hour, otherwise they would have to make a negative from the originals, and that was a twenty-four-hour process.

I then stopped at Dunhill's, on Post and Sutter, finding a vacant fire hydrant right in front of the building. As I was coming out of the store with a box of nicely wrapped cigars under my arm, a meter maid was pulling alongside my car. She got off her three-wheeler and looked skeptically at the box under my arm. Meter maids think that cops in general are lazy and overpaid. Plainclothes detectives rank several notches lower.

"It's not all red lights and sirens, you know," I said, as I hustled behind the wheel and got out of there before she could write a ticket.

I went to the Hall of Justice and flashed my badge to the bored-looking cop sitting behind the metal detector so I wouldn't have to wait in line behind the sad-looking lot of civilians combing through their pockets for keys, metal combs, compacts, cigarettes, knives, guns, or hand grenades—anything that might set off the delicate alarm system.

I walked to the fourth floor. I never take an elevator at the Hall of Justice if I can help it. It's not that I'm claustrophobic, it's just that the people that ride up and down in those things scare the hell out of me. At least on the stairs you can turn around and run the other way if one of the defendants on his way to or from a court date suddenly throws a wingding because of a slight miscalculation on his daily chemical intake.

Harry Saito was sitting behind his desk in the crime lab. I dropped the Dunhill's bag on the top of his overstuffed box for incoming mail.

He leaned over and peeked inside the bag, then gave me a big smile.

"All for me?"

"Yes."

"And what can I do for you, Mr. Polo?"

I handed him the styptic pencil I'd taken from Keith Chadway's medicine cabinet. I had a gut feeling the blood particles would turn out to be AB-negative, the same type found on Johnny Aiello's knife blade.

"I just want to know what type blood we have here."

His forehead washboarded into lines of suspicion. "A whole box of cigars for just that?"

"I'd like the information as soon as possible."

Saito opened the bag, unwrapped the box and pried it open, picked out a cigar, and ran it under his nose. "Call me in half an hour," he said, taking out his pocketknife and scraping the dried blood from the styptic pencil.

I walked down the hall to homicide. Tehaney was at his desk. He had a brown paper bag in front of him.

"Just having lunch," he said, taking a round container of cottage cheese from the bag. "The coroner called in a preliminary report on North." He rummaged around the top of his desk, found the paper he wanted, and handed it to me.

"You should have been a doctor," I told him. "This looks like prescription writing. I can't understand a word of it."

He took the paper back and squinted at it. "You're right. Sometimes even I can't read the crap I write. Basically what we have is your old blunt instrument to the back of the head. Crushed his skull. Dead before he hit the water. Doc says he was pumped full of cocaine. Potrero station found his car, a Mercedes, parked out by Candlestick Park. It couldn't have been there long, not with the tires still on it."

"So it's possible he was killed there and dumped into the bay," I said.

He pulled up the top of the cottage cheese container and skimmed off a scoop with a white plastic spoon.

"Possible. Also possible he could have been killed somewhere else, anywhere else, and driven over by Candlestick. I'm going out there after lunch and meet with the crime lab crew. Want to come along?"

"No, I don't think so."

He chewed on the cottage cheese, made a face, then took another spoonful. "Tastes like milk and sawdust."

"Why eat it?"

He patted his stomach. "Ulcers, Polo. Cases like this and guys like you. They give you ulcers." He held his stomach while he let out a low burp. "Keep in touch."

I stopped and picked up the photographs, then called Harry Saito from a pay phone.

"Type AB-negative, Nick," Saito said. "One of the rare ones. Shall I send you the test sheet?"

"It would be better for both of us if you just threw it away."

"I kind of thought so. Take care. Stop by any time you have an extra box of cigars."

It's about a four-hour drive from San Francisco to Reno. You can fly there in about forty-five minutes. Of course that entails a trip to the airport, half an hour, if there's no traffic problems. You've got to hope to find a parking space for your car, then you check in at least an hour before flight time so you don't get bumped, then there is the normal half hour wait, either at the boarding area, or in the plane on the taxi way, so, all in all, it about evens out. It's not that flying bothers me, not at all. It's those damn takeoffs and landings.

I stopped at my flat, packed a few clothes and some Sinatra, Basie, and Torme tapes, and pointed the car toward Reno.

When I pulled into the Fiesta's parking lot, I mentioned the name Uncle Pee Wee had given me, John Boscacci, and got the royal treatment. A bellboy took my one piece of luggage from the car and escorted me to the elevators. We went right to a room on the top floor, not

135

even bothering to check in. He deposited my bag in the middle of the king-sized bed and asked if everything was satisfactory. I thanked him and handed him a five-dollar bill. There were several unopened liquor bottles and a bucket of ice on a counter near the window. My view was of the neighboring Harrah's casino. I fixed a light Scotch and water and had taken my first sip when the phone rang.

"John Boscacci, Mr. Polo. Everything all right?"

"Just fine. I'd like to see you."

"Come on down. My office is in back of the cashier's cage."

Boscacci was a tall, straight-backed man in his forties, dressed in an immaculate dark blue suit. He had expensively barbered hair and the air of a man who knew what made the world go round.

I showed him the DMV photograph.

He put on a pair of horn-rimmed reading glasses and sat down behind his desk. "That's the guy. I paid him off personally. Any winnings that high I have to okay."

"Why did you give him cash?"

Boscacci shrugged. "He asked for cash." He took the glasses off and polished the lenses with the fat end of his tie. "Besides, when you give them cash, they're much more likely to start gambling with it right away. Giving us a chance to get some of it back."

"Is that what the man in the picture did?"

"No. Took off like a rabbit. Never saw him again."

I passed him the photograph of Dave Church. "Recognize this one?"

He put his glasses back on. "No. Any reason why I should?"

"The first picture is from a driver's license. It was

136

issued to James Widmer, the name of the man you gave all the cash to."

"Your uncle told me that Widmer had died months ago."

"Right. Someone had his license reissued. I've got a hunch it's that kid in the other picture."

Boscacci held the photographs together. "Could be, I guess. Can I keep these?"

"Sure. Wasn't it a little unusual for someone to be betting so much money on one race?"

"We were having our Thoroughbred handicapping tournament. It's a three-day event. Top prize is two hundred and fifty thousand dollars. We were mobbed and there were a lot of high rollers around."

"But the bet scared you enough to call and try and get the odds dropped."

Boscacci finished polishing his glasses and slipped them in his coat pocket, careful not to mess the neatly pointed handkerchief. "Sure. We called. It's automatic in a situation like that. This is a business. It's like the stock market. There's someone called a specialist that works right on the market floor. He specializes in just one stock. His job is to see that the fluctuations aren't too wide or excess in his stock. If his stock happens to drop off too fast, he'll buy some himself, just to keep the market in that stock up. It's all very professional and legal. I don't see much difference in what we do. We're all businessmen, trying to avoid big losses." His eyes narrowed, like a cat's. "Losing the money is no big deal, Mr. Polo. Being made to look foolish is. And Mr. Aiello's death makes it personal. He didn't work for us directly, and I didn't know the man, but we've done business with your uncle for years. We're offering a twenty-five thousand dollar reward for information leading to the identification of whoever was responsible.''

"Is the information for you, or for the police?''

"That depends. We always like to see the police handle these matters when possible.''

I took out the cheap ballpoint I found in Dave Church's pants pocket.

"I've got a possible lead on the man in the picture. He may have stayed at the Sundial Motel.''

Boscacci took a gold pen from his coat pocket and wrote the motel's name down on a pad of paper bearing the Fiesta's logo. "I don't know anyone there personally, but I'll make a call.'' He looked at his watch. "It's a little late. Maybe you should talk to them tomorrow.'' He stood up and extended his hand. "Meanwhile, you're our guest here. I've made reservations for you at the penthouse restaurant and the late show. Enjoy yourself.''

I did. Dinner was definitely enjoyable. The show consisted of a group of impersonators doing everyone from Monroe to Truman Capote, and was passable. I played blackjack and craps for a couple of hours, more or less, breaking even, more or less.

It was a few minutes after ten in the morning when I got to the Sundial Motel. The clerk was a reed-thin middle-aged guy with a sour expression and a badly pockmarked face. I introduced myself and got a grunt. The name John Boscacci did wonders for his expression.

"Yes, sir. How can I help?''

I showed him the two pictures and explained I wanted to know if either of the gentlemen had been a guest on the twenty-fifth or twenty-sixth of last month.

"Martha,'' he called out, and a heavyset woman with bleached white hair and a bright blue jump suit came to

138

the desk. "This is my wife," the man explained. "We were both working those days."

Martha made a rumbling noise. "We both work every damn day, mister. It's no picnic running a place like this, believe me."

I believed her. They both looked at the pictures carefully. Martha put a stubby finger on the picture of David Church. "That's the cute kid that was staying in room 412, isn't it, honey?"

Honey shook his head. "Damned if I remember him."

"I can't be sure, but it kind of looks like him," Martha said, bending down and pulling out a small clear plastic box. She started thumbing through registration cards, stopping to pull one out. "Here it is," she said, as if she was waving a winning raffle ticket. "Room 412."

She handed me the card. It definitely wasn't a winning ticket.

"Jim Smith," I read out loud.

"We rent rooms, mister," the man said. "We don't have to check out who they are, as long as they pay."

"Don't tell me, let me guess. This guy paid by cash."

He took the card back. "Yep, says so right here."

"And I didn't see a car license."

"Probably took the bus," Martha said brightly. "Lots of people do that."

Jim Smith had scribbled his name and an address that looked like 782 Market Street, San Francisco. It could have been 762, and it could have easily been Mason Street.

There was a small Canon copy machine behind the counter. Martha made me a copy of the card while I dug

139

through the other registration slips for the twenty-fifth &
twenty-sixth. Nothing there of much interest, unless you
consider the fact that there were three other Jim Smiths
listed as guests of the motel on those dates.

I tried to make some sense of it on the drive home.
Johnny Aiello presumably stabbed one of his attackers before he died. The attacker had an AB-negative blood
type, according to Sergeant Eller. Chadway had a bandage
on his arm, and the sample from his styptic pencil showed
AB-negative blood. That is a rare blood type, but there're
probably hundreds of thousands of people with it. Big
deal. Chadway could explain away the cut on his arm a
hundred different ways.

And why would Chadway get involved in fixing a
race? His father was rich with a capital *R*. Forbes 500 rich.
Was Daddy going to cut him off? The kid looked like he
was in charge of the stud farm the day I was there. So why
would a kid like that take a flyer on a horse race?

Dave Church might have some answers, but he was
in Europe. "Somewhere between Paris and Nice." A nice
somewhere to be, especially since at the moment, I was
nowhere.

When I got home there was a message from Jane Tobin saying that she wouldn't be able to make dinner that
night.

I called Bob Tehaney, but he was out. I caught
Lieutenant Gallegos at his office.

"Lieutenant, I showed that DMV photograph to the
people at the Reno casino. It was the same man who
made the bet and picked up the money. Did you get a
look at the picture?"

"Yes, and the date of issue too. From what you told

me, James Widmer was in no condition to have his picture taken at that time."

"No, and there's no resemblance between the DMV photo and the picture that Widmer's brother gave me of James. Did Bob Tehaney call you about Bobby North?"

"Yeah, he told me about the Coast Guard finding his body in the bay. It's a real mystery, isn't it, Polo? But that's what we get paid to solve, me and Tehaney, by the taxpayers. Keep in touch."

I made a cup of espresso and started mixing names in my mind. Bobby North, Chadway, Church, Donald Jepson, Leo Goens, Connie Jepson. Connie Jepson. I wandered into my office and found the notebook with her phone number on it. She answered on the eighth ring.

"Mrs. Jepson, this is Inspector Polo, I spoke to you the other night, I—"

"Oh, yes, Inspector. Could you hang on a moment please? I just got out of the shower."

The thought of Connie Jepson getting out of the shower brought a smile to my face, until I thought about Leo Goens maybe being in there with her. No. No way. They don't make showers that big.

She came back on the line a few minutes later.

"Sorry to keep you waiting, Inspector. I tried calling you at that number you gave me, but there was something wrong. All I ever got was a recording saying the number wasn't working."

"Yes, they're doing some remodeling down here, all kinds of problems with the phones. Why were you calling, Mrs. Jepson?"

"Connie, please call me Connie. I was digging through some of Donald's papers, and I think I found something about that company you asked me about. Alta or Alpha something?"

"The Alta Group?"

"Yes, that's the one."

"I'd like to stop down and see you, Connie."

"I've got a business appointment in a few minutes. Could we make it later tonight? Down at the ranch. I have to do some work there, and that's where the papers are."

"Fine, what time's good for you?"

"Say about eight o'clock?"

The same time I was supposed to meet her late husband. "Fine, I'll be there."

20

I made a couple of tuna and tomato sandwiches, put them in a bag with a banana and an apple and a half-bottle of red wine, made sure the .38 was safely snuggled in the car's headrest, and by six o'clock I was parked under a strand of eucalyptus trees a quarter-mile or so down from the gate leading to the Jepson ranch.

At five after seven a white Buick coupe, with Connie Jepson alone at the wheel, stopped at the gate. Connie undid the lock, then drove into the ranch. I waited until a few minutes after eight, drained the last sip of the wine, and headed into the ranch.

The Buick, parked right in front of the house, was the lone vehicle in sight.

Connie Jepson was waiting for me at the lighted front door. She had on white slacks and a white top with silver sequins on it. She looked like she was ready to get up on stage and belt out a song.

"Nice to see you again," she said, putting out her

hand. She gripped my hand firmly. A little too firmly. I saw a blur out of the corner of my eye, then something hard and heavy hit the side of my head. The floor was rushing up to meet my face, but I didn't have the strength to put my arms out to stop the fall. I remembered hearing a sickening crunching sound, then nothing.

My whole right side felt numb when I came to, and there was the taste of blood in my mouth. I shook my head as gently as possible and spat out some blood.

"You're going to ruin the carpet doing that, asshole."

I squinted through one eye and saw the imposing figure of Leo Goens sitting on the sofa. Standing next to him was Keith Chadway. He had a bullwhip coiled around his right shoulder. His smile looked like it was etched on with a razor blade.

"Nice to see you again, Mr. Polo," Chadway said.

I tried to put a hand to my aching head, but found that both hands were tied behind my back.

"Leo, what the hell's going on?" I said, the words coming out mushy and garbled. My throat felt like it was lined with sandpaper.

Leo stood up and came over and lifted me to my feet. As soon as he let go, I sank back down to the floor again.

"You don't take much of a punch, do you, pretty boy?"

I tried to think of a clever response, but all I could come up with was, "Fuck you."

Goens smiled, showing freckled teeth. He picked me up again and dragged me over to the couch.

"I didn't see you guys come in. Been here all day?" I asked.

"There's a back road dummy. Couldn't use a car,

but with a bike, or a horse, no problem. We figured you'd be smart enough to stake out the place."

My eyes were starting to focus. Leo was wearing his usual Levi's, leather vest, and bloated flesh.

Chadway was dressed in a cowboy outfit: dusty jeans, a denim jacket with a red corduroy collar, thin black leather gloves, and a straw hat tipped down over his forehead.

"Boys, if you wanted to talk, all you had to do was ask. Why all the rough stuff?"

"Shut up," Leo said.

Connie Jepson came into the room. She looked down at me with sorry eyes.

"Is he going to be all right?"

"What difference does it make?" Chadway said. "Let's take him outside where there's more room."

Leo lifted me off the couch with one massive arm and carried me out to the back of the house, toward the barn. We passed a black and white saddled horse and a big Harley Davidson motorcycle.

"Tie him to the fence," Chadway said.

Leo looped a leather harness attached to the fence through the knots on my hands and pulled it tight.

Chadway was some ten or fifteen feet away. He unrolled his whip and sent it snapping my way. I winced as it tore a gouge out of the fence.

"That's just to get your attention, Polo. I want to ask you a few questions, and how you answer them . . ." he snapped the whip out again, and it came an inch or two closer to my shoulder. "How truthfully you answer them will determine the amount of pain you're going to suffer. Now tell me just how much you've been telling the police about me."

145

"Nothing," I said.

The damn whip cracked and if I hadn't had my shoulders hunched in, it would have taken a slice off.

"Don't lie, Polo."

"I'm not lying. I haven't even mentioned your name to the cops."

"But you have been talking to them, haven't you, asshole," Leo Goens said.

He was standing to my left, his arm around Connie Jepson's shoulders. She was shaking, and her eyes were dancing with excitement or fear, I didn't know which.

"Yes, of course I've spoken to them. And I mentioned your name, Leo. They know all about you, and what's going on up at the Whipcord."

"And just exactly what is that?" Chadway asked.

"Running dope."

Chadway and Leo exchanged smiles.

"Tell me more," Chadway said.

"A Lieutenant Gallegos, the one who came to Jepson's ranch to investigate his death, he mentioned to me that they thought that Leo was selling dope, that's all."

Chadway dragged the whip back slowly, coiling it in a circle. It was an ugly-looking thing, tapering black braided leather with a thick handle. It must have been at least twelve feet long.

"And what else did you and Gallegos talk about?" he asked, flexing the whip between his hands.

"We talked a little about a bookie, Bobby North. He's dead. They found him floating in San Francisco Bay."

"And who do they think killed poor Bobby?"

"They haven't a clue. A bookie like that, he'd have a lot of enemies."

146

"And you never mentioned my name even once?" Chadway said.

"No."

He laughed. Giggled might be more like it. "You're not very convincing. Not convincing at all. I think you have to be . . . stimulated, to get you to tell the truth. Connie, unzip Mr. Polo's pants."

"Keith, I don't want—" she protested.

Leo put a ham hand on her shoulder and pushed her toward me. "Do it," he said.

Connie walked hesitantly toward me and unzipped my pants.

"Pull out his dick," Chadway ordered.

Her fingers fumbled clumsily, but she finally got the job done.

"Not much of a target, is there?" Chadway asked Goens and they both laughed.

Chadway walked over and looked into my eyes. "Did you ever see that old circus trick, Polo? Where they blindfold a pretty girl, put a lighted cigarette in her mouth, and then some handsome young man, usually dressed in black silk, takes a big whip and just knocks the cigarette out of her mouth without touching her." His hand grabbed my face and squeezed. "Have you seen that trick? Because we're going to try it right now, but instead of a cigarette, we're going to use your cock." He let go of my face and backed off a few feet. "But as good as I am with this whip, I'll need a bigger target. Connie, get him hard."

"I don't—"

"Suck his cock, darling. Get it nice and hard."

Connie edged away. "No, why don't you do it, you'll—"

147

The whip snapped out and wrapped around her right boot. She squealed in pain and looked to Leo for help.

"Suck it, baby. Do like he says," Leo said.

She started to cry, then dropped to her knees and engulfed my penis in her mouth. It wasn't very difficult. Terror does strange things to you in a situation like this. A hummingbird probably could have swallowed what was there.

"I'm telling you, Chadway, I never mentioned your name to the police."

Connie sobbed and pulled her head away. "Please, Leo, I can't—"

"Shut up, you bitch," Chadway screamed, then sent the whip out toward Connie Jepson.

Her head started bobbing up and down like a woodpecker. She looked up at me. Tears were running in curvy lines through her makeup. Her eyes were ringed in gray like an unrinsed bath.

"For God's sake, let the lady alone. And if that's the same whip you used on the horse that killed Jepson, you'd better put it away. Whip marks are like fingerprints, and the cops can trace them just as easily." I had no idea if that was true, but it certainly was an inspired piece of bullshit if it wasn't. I could see the doubt forming in Chadway's eyes. "Besides, I didn't tell the cops about you for a very good reason. There's a twenty-five thousand dollar reward out for whoever ripped off the Fiesta Casino on the Trish's Lamb Chop race."

"Reward? Who put out a reward?" demanded Goens.

"The casino. They don't like being ripped off, and they're not too happy about their man being killed at the track."

"And you think I'm responsible?" Chadway said, running the whip between his fingers.

"Yes, you and Dave Church. I think you did it, I just don't know why."

Chadway strolled over and patted Connie Jepson on the shoulder. "You can get up now, darling." He fondled the whip's handle, held it in front of my eyes, then brought it down hard and fast right into my groin.

I cried out, and if the ropes weren't holding me up I would have fallen to the ground. It took some time for the tears to stop streaming, and when I did open my eyes Chadway was waving the whip handle in front of me again.

"Think the police can trace those marks, asshole?" he said, then hit me again.

If there was any difference in the intensity of the pain, there was no way I could tell. Even though it hurt my tied hands like hell, my legs simply wouldn't hold me up, and I slumped down and forward, flashes of red and white exploding across my eyelids.

"Untie him please, Leo," Chadway said.

When the knots were loosened I slid to the ground, falling on my side, bringing my knees up to my chin. I dug my fingers into my kneecaps and rocked back and forth.

Chadway crouched down beside me and peeled back one of my eyelids.

"My, my, Mr. Polo. You look like you need a drink. What will it be? Bourbon? Is that all right with you? Connie, go and fetch us a bottle."

I lay there, trying to shake some of the pain away.

149

"Just what makes you so sure that Dave Church and I were involved with that horse race?" Chadway said.

"James Widmer's driver's license was used as identification to pick up the winnings. But Widmer was already dead. You had access to his mail. You could have had Church go and get a new license issued under Widmer's name. Jepson told me that Sam Vickers was handling all the paper work for the horse's owners, the Alta Group. Vickers is your attorney. You train horses. Dave Church had a pile of racing forms in his room. It all added up. I just couldn't figure out a reason."

"And have you told the people in Reno your suspicions?"

"No, I was still trying to work things out." The pain was subsiding now. I struggled to a sitting position and leaned back against the fence.

Connie Jepson came rushing back with a bottle and glass in her hand.

"Good girl," Chadway said, taking the bottle and pouring until the glass was half-filled. He handed it to me.

"Seems a shame to waste good booze on this asshole," Leo Goens said.

I took a sip, then looked at the label. Wild Turkey.

"It won't be wasted, Leo," Chadway said. "Believe me. Drink up, Polo. You've got a long way to go." He topped off the glass with more of the whiskey. "Drink, man, or Leo will have to pour it down your throat."

I took a deep drink, then said, "Why, Chadway? Why would a man like you, with your money, bother fixing a horse race?"

"You've read too many cornball novels, Polo, where the hero is in a tight fix and gets the villain to tell him just why he did his dastardly deeds, then the hero effects a

150

miraculous escape. It doesn't happen that way in real life. Just shut up and drink."

He grabbed me by the hair and pulled my head back, then poured some whiskey down my throat right from the bottle. I swallowed some and spat some out. Chadway slapped me hard across the face with his gloved hand.

"We're in a hurry. Drink, man!" he shouted.

I took a swallow from the glass in my hand and he immediately topped it off again.

No one said a word for the next five or so minutes. I'd sip some of the booze, swallow hard, and get more in the glass.

Finally Chadway said, "He's getting close, Leo. Finish him up. I'll get things ready." He grabbed Connie Jepson by the elbow, whispered something in her ear and pulled her with him toward the house.

Leo bent over me and pushed the glass in my face. "Not really too bad a way to go out, huh, Polo? A blow job and a heat on. Swallow that booze."

21

I had to agree with him in a way. Of course, I was thinking of going out under the influence of expensive champagne, in the arms of a beautiful woman while I was celebrating my ninety-fifth birthday.

"Just how am I going to die?" I asked Leo.

"You're going for a short ride in your car, asshole. You're going to hit a big redwood tree. You're going to splatter yourself all over the windshield. You shouldn't drink when you drive, don't you know that?"

I took in a big mouthful of the bourbon and pretended to swallow, then held up my glass for a refill. Leo bent over to fill my glass, and when he was at face level I sprayed the whiskey from my mouth at his eyes then jammed the glass into his throat. It broke off and I pulled it back and shoved the jagged remains toward his nose.

Leo grabbed his throat and screamed and I pushed myself to my feet. The nearest transportation was Leo's motorcycle, but even if I found the key, I'd never get far in it. That left Chadway's horse. My fingers fumbled trying to untie the reins from the fence, but I finally got it done, then approached the horse from the left side. I knew that much, get on on the left side. He kept edging away while my foot groped for the stirrup. I finally got the foot in, then pulled myself up. The last time I'd been in a saddle was when my father had taken me on a pony ride in the zoo.

Leo Goens came running at us, his face a mask of blood. He grabbed the horse's reins and pulled them from my hand. The horse started to buck. I grabbed his mane and dug my heels into his side. He started galloping. At least I guess that's what you'd call it. All I know is that my fanny and the saddle were out of rhythm, and every time I'd be coming down, the saddle was coming up.

Goens was screaming, then came the gunshots. I twisted my head back and saw Chadway running our way. The horse didn't need any encouraging now. The gunshots spooked him and we took off fast, bam, bam, bam, the saddle hitting my ass now like, you'll excuse the expression, a pile driver.

Things were rushing by: trees, posts. We were away from the lighted area now. It was a clear night, with enough moonlight to give me an idea of what we were headed for, a fence.

No matter how many cowboy movies you've seen where the guy yells, "Whoa," and the horse pulls up, believe me, it doesn't work. I "Whoaed" my head off, but we just kept picking up speed. I had a death grip on the horse's mane and my face was buried in his neck. I peeked up and saw the fence getting closer and closer. I switched from "Whoa" to another old favorite of mine, "Giddyup." I could have recited the Gettysburg Address for all the difference it made to this horse. He had a mind of his own. I managed a weak, "Hi ho, Silver" as he started his leap. I don't know how we made it, because my eyes were closed tight. I had the feeling of flying free, then we hit the ground and I was bounced all over the place, but my grip on his mane somehow kept me in the saddle. He kept galloping like hell. We crossed a paved road, and headed into a wooded area. Branches snapped at my face and I went back to "Whoa" again. Then we were back on a paved road. I saw headlights coming right at us. I looked for a soft spot on the side of the road to fall off on. The horse seemed to be slowing down. Maybe he was tiring. I know I was. More headlights. The horse seemed startled and made for another fence. I heard a crack as he jumped, his hooves must have hit a railing. I went flying and came down in a pile of tall weeds. I lay there panting like a locomotive, feeling around for broken bones. There didn't seem to be any, but every muscle I owned pro-tested when I moved. Especially the cheeks of my ass.

I rolled to my side and got to my knees. The horse was long gone, thank the Lord. I was lying not more than ten feet from the fence, which was right next to a road. If I'd been sober, the fall probably would have killed me. Every couple of minutes headlights would appear. They looked wonderful, until it dawned on me that either Leo or Chadway might be in one of the cars, looking for me.

I tried to get my bearings. There were what looked to be a thousand or more trees: bushy pines, all evenly spaced out, graduating in size from no more than saplings, to eight-footers. A Christmas tree farm. I crawled into the line of bigger trees and collapsed. I remember humming a few lines from *Silent Night*, before passing out.

154

22

I don't know how long I was out. It was still dark. I maneuvered my watch around until there was enough light to read the dials. Two-twenty in the morning. I got to my feet in stages, inches at a time, groaning aloud as muscles and joints screamed at me to lie back down again.

I hobbled over to the fence, bent over like Quasimodo. It was only four or so feet high, but right now it looked like the Berlin Wall. I figured out a better way, dropped to my knees and started to crawl under the damn thing.

Something made an odd noise and there were rustling sounds, an animal of some kind. Of the kind I didn't want to meet. I limboed under the fence and cautiously made my way up to the road. I kept to one side, ready to jump into the brush at the first sight of a car.

I walked for about fifteen minutes. Things were starting to look a little familiar. I passed by the spot where I had parked and staked out the Jepson ranch. I moved deeper into the brush. When I got across from the entrance to Jepson's ranch I waited a few minutes, then scooted over to the gate. The big padlock was in place again, which meant they were either locked in or out for the night. I didn't plan on finding out which.

I continued down the road, knowing that eventually it would take me into Woodside.

I was almost on top of the car before I saw it. It was off the side of the road, nosed against a big tree. It had a big whip antenna. I did my Davy Crockett bit back in the brush for several minutes. The only sounds were crickets and something howling in the distance.

It would be a perfect trap. Old Polo stumbling along, seeing his car and running up to it, only to find big Leo and Keith and his wonder whip. I waited a good ten minutes. Nothing. It dawned on me that they would have no idea that I'd be walking down this road. As far as they knew I could be still atop Old Paint, riding west, or have fallen off and broken my neck. There was no way they could figure I'd be hiking this way. And what if a sheriff's car came by? They wouldn't want to be anywhere near the damn car.

I waited another ten minutes. Still nothing. I crept up to the car. There was no one in the front seat. No one in the back seat. I opened the door and went right for the head rest, pulling the .38 belly gun out. The keys were in the ignition. I tried them. The motor turned sluggishly and I nursed the engine to life. I put it in reverse and backed up slowly. We hit a ditch of some kind and the car wouldn't go back any farther. I rocked it between drive and reverse for a couple of minutes, finally got some traction on the back tires, and backed it up on the road. One of those damn idiot lights came on the dash, a little red symbol of an oil can. I watched it nervously all the way to Jane Tobin's apartment.

"It looks a little like a Jackson Pollock abstract painting, Nick, all those little blue, black, and red blotches," Jane Tobin said.

"Thanks. You really know how to cheer a guy up."

She spread some warm oil on my buttocks and gently began to rub it in. "I think you're the first man I've ever told that his tush was a work of art."

"You *think* I'm the first?" I groaned as she wiped off the excess oil with a towel.

"Turn over, sissy," she said.

I did so, slowly and painfully. When I was flat on my back, she said, "Oh, he hurt you down there too, didn't he? Poor little guy."

I glanced down. "You're very spoiled since seeing that jockey."

"You were lucky, Nick, really. I don't know how you survived."

"I owe it all to a hollow leg. They didn't know they were dealing with a professional drunk."

"I still think you should go to the police."

"And do what? Tell them my side of the story? Chadway, Goens, and Connie Jepson would just deny it."

"You've got to do something."

"Yes, and I'll need your help."

I called Mrs. Damonte and told her that Jane was coming over, and that I'd appreciate it if she let her in my flat, through the back door. I told Jane what I needed.

"Bring a big purse. Go in through Mrs. Damonte's, go up to my place, and go back out through her front door."

"Do you actually think someone is watching your place?"

"I don't know. I do know that Chadway and Leo must be curious, and nervous as hell. I want to keep them that way for a while. If you see anyone watching you, or think you're being tailed, just drive off to work and call me from there, okay? Remember, these people are crazy, so be careful."

I handed her the .38. "Take this with you." She hefted the gun in one hand, then broke open the cylinder, saw that it was loaded, snapped it back in place, and nodded. "I can take care of myself." She gave me a mocking glance. "Unlike some people I know."

I was learning more about her hidden talents every day. She picked up a canvas purse big enough to hold the trade imbalance, in small bills, poured me a full cup of coffee, and took off.

Since I wasn't going to be able to use my computer, I'd have to use someone else's. The police department's computer had a lot more going for it than my data base did. It was able to pick up driver's licenses without having the license number or subject's date of birth. I called Inspector Paul Paulsen, an old buddy, and asked him to run DMV checks on Chadway, Goens, and Connie Jepson. "I'd like to check both their licenses and see how many cars they own, Paul."

"Okay, Nick. I'll have it in a couple of hours," Paulsen said.

Next I called a garage I'd done business with before and arranged for them to work on my car. The final call was to a rental agency that specialized in trucks.

I called Connie Jepson's house. No answer. Telephone information gave me a number for the Chadway ranch. The rough voice that answered said "young Chadway" wasn't around. Telephone information had no listing for a Leo Goens.

After I put down the phone I soaked in Jane's tub, then took a hot shower, dressed in my rather grubby clothes, and felt reasonably well by the time she got back.

She started unloading her bag.

"That nice lady made me take some food," she said, placing a aluminum foil–covered pie plate on the table. I lifted the foil and inhaled. Artichoke heart frittata. Heaven. The other two items in her purse were a .25 Beretta in an ankle holster, and a four-inch barrel .357 Magnum in a shoulder rig.

Guns are evil, no doubt, but a necessary evil, I told myself, trying to get the massive shoulder holster in a somewhat comfortable position. The Magnum was issued to me when I joined the police department. When you first become a cop, and you're all gung ho, you don't mind the forty-four ounces of metal flopping on your hip or under your shoulder. You even get a "backup" gun, like the little Beretta, and keep it in an ankle holster, or in your front pocket, so you can hold it in your hand when the weirdos walk up to you and ask unusual questions. Then you get tired of packing all that weight, so you go to a slightly smaller gun, maybe a .9 mm automatic. Then, when and if you become a detective, one of the snub nose .38 revolvers seems to be the best bet. But even that damn thing gets heavy, so you wind up just carrying something small and light, like the little Beretta.

I clipped the ankle holster on.

"Getting ready to go to war, are we?" Jane asked.

"This is just in case you fight me for the last piece of the frittata."

After we ate Jane followed me to the garage. The mechanic took one look and smiled, figuring he might be able to charge enough to take the wife and kiddies down to Carmel for a few days.

He was disappointed when I told him all I wanted was the oil problem fixed and the hood straightened out.

"But this thing is a mess. I can prime it all out and paint it for you. It'll look like new."

There was no sense explaining that was the last thing I wanted. I took the Swiss Army knife from the glove compartment, and my camera, maps, and binoculars from the car's trunk.

Jane drove me to the truck rental place. I found just what I wanted. A four-wheel drive pickup, with a camper shell.

"What are you going to do now?" Jane asked, while I waited for the truck's papers.

"If you were Leo and Chadway, what would you be doing right now?"

"Wondering about you, of course."

"And if I didn't show up?"

She screwed up one side of her face as if she were looking through a telescope. "Well, I might think we scared you off, or maybe you died, or . . ."

"What about Connie Jepson?"

Both eyes screwed up now. "What about her?"

"She's the weak link, Jane. When Leo and Chadway aren't worrying about me, I'll bet they're worrying about her."

23

I drove downtown, and, since I no longer had my ticket-evader, had to park in a garage. My first stop was the costume shop, where I picked up two mustaches: one short and thin, the other a bushy devil that I was afraid would tickle my nose.

Next I went to the Emporium, bought a pair of pre-washed, preshrunk, and, from the looks of them, pre-owned Levi's, a couple of cotton sport shirts, underwear, socks, and a black Members Only jacket. I changed into the new clothes as I was buying them. My Italian loafers had taken a beating, so I picked up a pair of black Reeboks. They didn't have any cowboy hats. The salesman recommended a western wear store on Valencia Street, so I drove out to the Mission District and picked up one of those white straw jobs, making me look somewhat like a reject from a Marlboro ad.

I drove to the Hall of Justice, and, minus the hat, went up to the robbery detail and met Paul Paulsen.

"The casual look is coming back, huh, Nick?" was all he said when he handed me the computer printouts. I took them back to the truck and studied them. Connie Jepson's DMV showed her with the ranch address, and she had no cars registered under her name. They must have been registered to poor old Donald Jepson.

Keith Chadway's record showed him with one Porsche, and his listed residence was the family home in Hillsborough.

Leo Goens's home address was shown as 642 7th Lane, South San Francisco. He had four different motorcycles and a '79 Ford pickup registered to him.

I did a little more shopping, picking up a thermos bottle, a sleeping bag and microcassette player-recorder with a built in dubber, so you could copy the tapes you just made. All this and an AM-FM radio in a package the size of a paperback book.

I stopped at a delicatessen, ordered two roast beef and cheddar sandwiches on sourdough French rolls, filled up the thermos, and headed for South San Francisco.

You can always tell the neighborhood drug dealer. He's the one with the thick iron bars covering his house. Always the best protected place on the block. Goens's was no exception. It was an old frame home, chalky beige with faded white trim, set back from the street, with an exposed front stairway. There were thick oil and grease stains covering the driveway and tracked halfway up the front steps. With all the grillwork on the doors and windows, it looked like it could survive a full-fledged assault from Hagar the Horrible.

Goens's dark blue pickup truck was parked in the driveway, but that didn't necessarily mean he was home. Last night he was driving his motorcycle.

There was a gas station around the corner. I called a contact with the phone company, and five minutes later I was fifty dollars poorer, but had the telephone number for Goens's address. I called and let it ring twenty times. No answer.

I tried Connie Jepson's number again. Another no answer.

I drove out to Westlake, stopping along the way to call the Jepson number. Still nobody home. Or at least no one picking up the phone.

I parked up the street from her house. The Daly City weather was at its usual summer best. Pea soup fog. I got in the back, camper-shell part of the truck, stretched out on the sleeping bag, and waited. I went through both of the sandwiches and the coffee. When it was dark enough, I put on the cowboy hat and walked over to the house. None of the neighbors seemed interested.

Connie's front door was warped from the weather, and even after I had raked the lock with the Swiss Army knife I had to use my shoulder to push the door in.

There was that all-too-familiar smell of death right away. How do you describe that smell? A mixture of spoiling flesh and old excrement. "The final dump," as the ambulance attendants so coldly describe it. Mother nature making its last call on our urinary and colon tracks. She was in her bedroom, fully dressed in the same white slacks and sequined top she had been wearing the night before. She even had her shoes on. There was an empty glass and a bottle of Mumm's champagne on the dresser. The glass had a lipstick smear around the rim. The same glossy red lipstick that Connie had been wearing the first time I saw her. Now her lips were a dull pink. The champagne bottle was nearly empty. Lying on its side next to it

163

was a prescription drug bottle. A few yellow and red capsules spilled out onto the dresser top.

I touched her carotid artery and got nothing but the feel of cold, clammy skin.

One thing you learn when you're a cop and deal with death is that when people die, they leave expressions on their faces: fear, hate, pain, shock, surprise, whatever. It isn't until they get to the funeral parlor and the mortician pats them into place that they get that peaceful, wake-me-when-dinner's-ready look. Connie's face was rigid, set almost in a frown, as if she were worrying about something when she took that last breath.

I backed out to the doorway and stared at her. There was no note, of course. No final words for poor Connie. I wondered if they made her swallow the pills, or if they just dissolved them in the wine, then put the pill bottle out for display. Had she lain there sipping away, knowing what was coming? Had she been too scared to ask a question while she was told to have another drink, hoping that they weren't really planning to kill her, or had they threatened her with some excruciatingly painful form of torture, so that the pills looked like the easy way, the only way, out? I wondered if she was religious, if she believed in some kind of god, if she was given the opportunity to say a last prayer; the final plea bargain.

I walked back over and looked at her wrists and neck closely. No bruising, no scratching. "No visible scars," the coroner's report would read. None visible, but they were there. I bent down and mumbled a few quick Hail Marys and Our Fathers.

Aiello, Jepson, North, and now Connie. Two bookies and two losers. Not exactly the types of victims who had much influence in life, even less in death. The homicide conviction rate around here is about sixty percent. I mean sixty percent of the people who murder other people are identified, arrested, and convicted of their crimes. And most of these aren't exactly Agatha Christie–type murders. Nothing classy, nothing sophisticated: husbands strangling wives, wives knifing husbands, buddies with one or two too many getting in an argument over the ball game and pulling out guns. The sad fact is that if most murderers weren't outright stupid, or up to their eyes in drugs, they wouldn't get caught. And Chadway certainly wasn't stupid.

I took a quick look around the house. There was no sign of Connie's little dog. The Buick was parked in the garage with the keys in the ignition.

I kept my pace nice and slow as I walked back to the truck. The fog was even thicker now, so even if someone did notice me, they wouldn't be able to give much of a description.

There was no fog down by the Whipcord. Another balmy summer night. The parking lot was half-filled, mostly with pickups and motorcycles again. I checked all the bikes' license plates and found one matching the list on Goens's DMV records.

I donned a mustache, the bushy one. I was wrong, it didn't tickle a bit. I pulled the hat as low as it would go and peeked in the Whipcord's swinging doors. Leo was behind the bar. I was happy to see the bandages on his neck and face.

I waited in the truck, trying to keep my mind blank, the way cons do to make time go by without pain. The lot started emptying out, truck by truck, bike by bike. When Leo's was the only bike left, I made sure I had the cassette recorder in my jacket pocket, then went in through the back door, past the office where I'd met Donald Jepson, and then into the bar. I waited a few minutes, watching Leo puttering around behind the bar, moving bottles and glasses, and finally digging his stubby fingers into the cash register.

He didn't see me until I was leaning against the bar rail.

"We're closed, buddy. Take a hike," he said, barely glancing at me, then going back to the register.

"Cut yourself shaving, fatso?"

He swiveled around slowly, disbelief on his face. He started to come around the bar when he saw the Magnum pointed at his stomach.

"Hey, what the fuck is this, a hold up? I—"

"Don't play dumb, Leo, even though it's one of the few things in this life that you're good for." I took off the hat and mustache. "Great disguise, huh, Leo?"

He didn't say anything, just glared at me, with enough hate in his eyes to make him the next Ayatollah. I waved the Magnum. "Keep your hands up, and come over here."

He moved slowly, keeping those eyes on me all the time.

"Turn around," I said.

"Fuck you."

I walked over to the jukebox, dropped in a quarter, and punched a button without looking at the selection, keeping the gun trained on Leo all the while.

The music was all I could ask for: a loud mashing of electronic instruments doing battle with each other.

"Last chance, Leo. Turn around."

He got the "fuck" out, but before he had a chance to

attach the "you," I blew away at least one of the toes on his right foot.

He screamed and dropped to the ground, his hands grabbing at the blood-spurting boot. I slammed the butt of the gun against his head as hard as I could. Leo grunted and fell forward. I kicked him in the ribs, wishing I'd brought a pair of those pointed cowboy boots for the occasion. He was making moaning sounds, and I grabbed his ear and yanked until he sat up.

"Can you hear me, Leo?"

"You motherfu—"

I put the tip of the gun behind his ear lobe, the one with the silver earring, and pulled the trigger, blowing away the earring and the tip of the lobe. Leo screamed like a wounded elephant, one hand clutching his ear, the other holding onto his boot. He sat like that, moaning and sobbing. I walked over and unplugged the jukebox. No sense in torturing both of us.

There was a possibility that the gunshots would be reported to the police, but I doubted it. When the parking lot emptied out, there had been a steady stream of backfiring from the motorcycles and pickups. The nearest house was several hundred yards away, and they'd be used to all sorts of noises from the bar and the nearby freeway.

I went behind the bar and found a fairly clean bar rag. I brought it over and dumped it on Leo's lap.

"I'd work on the foot first. Stop the bleeding before you lose too much."

"You crazy bastard, I'm—"

"You're going to die, Leo, that's what you're going to do. You give me any more lip and I'm going to plug in the music again and start working my way up your leg until I get high enough to give you a vasectomy. Now wrap that around your foot."

He pulled off his boot and wrapped the towel around his toes. The towel turned from a dull gray to a bright red in a matter of seconds.

"Please, get me some help. I don't want to bleed to death."

I went behind the bar again and found a drawer stuffed with fresh towels. Leo wrapped several around his foot and held one over his ear.

I cocked the magnum and held the barrel against his left ear.

"Can you hear me okay?" I said.

"Yeah, I can hear okay, but I gotta see—"

"All you gotta do, Leo, is answer my questions. Answer them all, and there's a way out for you. You can still get away a free man, understand?"

He turned to look at me. There was no longer any hatred in his eyes. Just fear. I wondered when the last time was that Leo had fear in those dark eyes.

"First, who killed Johnny Aiello?"

"Who?"

"The old man at the racetrack."

"Oh, him. That was an accident. We were just going to put him out for a while. We—"

"Who is we?"

"Me and Chadway. Chadway had some drugs he was going to shoot into him to put him to sleep."

"What happened?"

"The old fart panicked, that's what happened. Keith went up to him, told him he knew Jepson and that he wanted to make a big bet. Keith told him he was worried about being seen passing the money. He suggested the men's room upstairs in the big place, where the high rollers go. I was waiting inside. We had an 'out of service' sign on the door, and as soon as they was inside, I put a wedge under the door. We dragged him onto the crapper, told him to take it easy. When Chadway started to stick him with the needle, he went ape. Pulled out that Mickey Mouse knife. I was holding his head. I just twisted it to get away from the knife. It was the old bastard's own fault, not mine."

I had no doubt that Goens actually thought it was poor old Johnny's fault.

"How did you and Chadway get together?"

"Through Don. Jepson. He was going nuts, losing dough, afraid Connie was going to dump him and take what he had left. The dumb bastard wanted me to kill her for him. Offered me two grand. I told him it would take a lot more. That's when he told me about the possible scam he had going on the fixed race. I told him I'd take care of Connie, if he let me in on the scam."

"So Jepson set you up with Chadway?"

"Yeah, but not right away. Jepson kept saying he was talking with his 'business partner.' Finally I met the guy, because they needed someone else at the track. Jepson didn't want to get involved with the old dude because he knew him. So I finally met Chadway and we set it up."

"Where?"

"At Jepson's ranch."

"Whose idea was it to kill Jepson?"

His fat face spread into an evil grin. "Kinda mutual consent. Jepson started shitting in his pants after the old bastard got killed. He would have a few drinks, start blubbering. He didn't mind if I bumped off his wife, but he got all upset about the old track guy. Then when you came here, I heard you talking to Jepson in his office. I called Chadway and told him about you."

"So who killed Jepson?"

He took in a deep breath and let the air out slowly. "Listen, you told me that I could get away from here. Now if I tell you this . . ."

I tapped him on the side of the head with the gun. "I meant what I said. Just answer the questions. Who killed Jepson?"

"Well, I guess we kinda both did. We got him drunk, then tossed him in with the horse. Chadway whipped the fucking horse until he went crazy, that's all."

That's all. Nice epitaph.

"What about Bobby North?"

"That asshole. He came around looking for Chadway's buddy, Church—the guy that made the bets with him. He wanted back all the money we'd won. Cheap cocksucker. He was down the college asking all kinds of questions. Chadway found out about it. That bookie didn't mind taking in the dough, but when he loses, he wants it back."

"But the race was fixed, wasn't it, Leo?"

"Sure, but we won. Who knows how many of those fucking races is fixed?"

A prison psychologist could spend a week with Leo and come out of the sessions a babbling idiot.

"Who killed him, Leo?"

"I did. The asshole threatened to go to the cops if we didn't come up with the dough. Imagine the dummy thinking we would believe that a bookie would go to the cops? Chadway set up a meeting. Fucking cokehead

170

shows up in his Merc, actually expecting us to fork it over. He thought he was a big man or something."

"What about Connie Jepson?"

"What about her?"

"Who killed her?"

"Connie's dead?" he asked almost innocently.

I bounced the barrel of the gun on his head.

"Hey, man. It wasn't me. After that fuckup at the ranch with you, I took off." His eyes started to look mean again. "I had to see a doc, get some stitches. Chadway took your car, Connie followed him. That's the last I saw of her."

Chadway must have dumped my car off the road, then taken off with Connie in her car.

"What was Connie's involvement?"

"Huh?"

"Connie, was she in on the fixed race?"

"No, dumb cunt. All she wanted to do was sing, become a singing star. She'd have humped a rhino if she thought it would help her."

"You seemed pretty friendly with her."

He grinned lewdly. "I told her about Jepson wanting to bump her off. She was scared shitless. When she was scared you could get her to do anything. She thought I was her protector."

"Did you talk to Chadway today?"

"You kidding? He must have called a half-dozen times asking about you. Had I heard from you? Heard anything about you? Had the cops been by? Shit like that."

After last night's episode I thought I'd never want to see a whiskey bottle again, but after listening to true confessions from Leo, I needed a drink. I went behind the bar, opened a fresh bottle of Jack Daniels, and took a swig. I carried the bottle back to Leo and put it at his feet.

"My turn to buy," I said, "but if you try anything funny, I'll blow a big hole in that belly of yours."

I took out the cassette recorder. Leo protested at first, but when I went over and plugged in the jukebox again, he agreed to be recorded.

It took some time. I'd ask a question, then push the switch on when he answered. The results were a choppy mix, but we got all the details down, and my voice was not on the finished tape. It would do. When we were finished I bent over the now half-drunk Leo Goens.

"Now, if you want to get out of this alive, here's what you'll have to do."

24

I left Leo to fend for himself, stopping in the parking lot just long enough to puncture both of his bike's tires with the blade from the Swiss Army knife.

I drove a mile or so, found a nice quiet spot by a new house under construction, crawled into the back of the truck, uncoupled my armament, and slipped into the sleeping bag. It was a little after three in the morning. I told my built-in alarm clock to wake me up at six. Unfortunately I woke up about every half hour, looked at my watch, then dozed off again.

By five-thirty I was back on the road. I stopped at the first Chevron gas station in sight, used the facilities, and, while washing up, wished I had thought to bring a toothbrush. The face looking back at me from the water-spotted mirror was unshaven, sullen, grim, even a little deranged. Perfect. I got back in the truck, and while driving slipped a blank cassette in the cassette recorder and made a copy of Leo's confessions. I had two copies made by the time I got to the post office at the airport. It's one of only two post offices in the state that is opened twenty-four hours a day, three hundred and sixty-five days a year. I made one more copy of the tape, then went in, bought some stamped envelopes, addressed one to myself at the flat and the other to myself in care of Uncle Pee Wee, then went back to the truck and headed for Hillsborough.

I was in luck. Keith Chadway's silver Porsche Carrera coupe was parked on the herringbone-patterned brick driveway, near the front of the house.

My rental truck had a big chrome trailer hitch on the back bumper. I maneuvered it around, then backed into the Porsche at about fifteen miles an hour.

I slipped the Beretta into the right-hand pocket of my jacket, the cassette player in the left, and got out and surveyed the damage. Probably about three hundred bucks to the truck and some three thousand to the Porsche. There was a large, jagged hole punched in the driver's side door.

By the time I got to the house the front door was opened by the same young Irish girl I'd met on my last visit. Instead of a maid's uniform, she was wearing a quilted bathrobe.

"Would you tell Keith that there's been an accident," I told her, putting my foot in the door. "Tell him Nick Polo is here."

Her eyes bounced from me to the damaged Porsche.

"Believe me," I said, pushing my way into the house, "he'll want to talk to me."

She tightened her robe tie. "Please wait here. I'll get Mr. Chadway."

"Here" was a tiled hallway leading to a wide car-

174

peted staircase, up which the young woman was now scurrying.

The walls were off-white, and they were covered with Impressionist paintings of rural villages and flower-filled hillsides. There were a half-dozen closed doors. The one that was opened led to a large rectangular room. One wall was all bookshelves from floor to ceiling, with little ladders running on tracks along the wall. Dark wooden beams crisscrossed the white plaster ceiling. Morning sun was muscling its way through the thinly curtained windows.

I heard the commotion and went back to the hallway. The young woman was hurrying down the stairs. Keith Chadway stood at the top railing and looked down at me.

I gave him a friendly wave.

"Seems I bumped into your car. Sorry about that."

"Are you alone?"

"Yes, all alone, and ready to deal."

He stared at me for a few moments, then said, "I'll be right down."

"Think I could get some coffee?" I asked the girl as she scooted past me.

I went into the room with the books and was glancing at the titles when Chadway entered.

"Just what the hell do you want?" he said.

He was wearing a silk robe, blue, with tiny red polka dots. His pale white legs showed under the robe. He had on a pair of dark leather slippers. His hair was uncombed and his high intelligent forehead was making high intelligent wrinkles. "It's money isn't it? How much?"

"How much are you offering?"

A shadow of a smile appeared on his face. "Just what

are *you* offering?" He had his right hand in his robe pocket. It looked full.

"You playing with yourself, or have you got a gun in there?" I asked.

"Do I need one?"

"Not for me."

The girl came into the room. She was back in uniform now, carrying a silver tray, with a silver coffee pot, two cups and saucers, and a little platter of cookies.

"The gentleman said he wanted coffee, Mr. Keith. Will you be wanting anything else?"

"No," Chadway snapped. "Go. Close the door. Leave. Go shopping or something."

"But I—"

"Leave, damn it!" he shouted.

She opened her mouth to protest, thought better of it, then turned on her heel and left, closing the door behind her.

"Don't get nervous now, Chadway. I'm going to reach in my jacket pocket and take out a tape recorder. I want you to listen to what's on it. Leo Goens's confession."

I eased the recorder out with two fingers, held it up, then tossed it toward him. He reached out for it, and I pulled out the Beretta. He juggled the recorder, and it hit the carpet with a dull thud.

"Just stay still," I said, as I walked over and reached into his robe pocket. It was a wicked-looking Walther automatic pistol. At least a thousand dollars retail. Real James Bond stuff. I had always wanted one.

I put the Beretta back in my pocket and pointed Chadway's gun at him.

"Pick up the machine. Play the tape."

176

He flopped into a high-back wing chair, like a runner whose legs had gone out on him. He didn't say a word while Goens's taped voice filled the room. When it was over his mood seemed to brighten.

"That isn't worth shit. It was obviously taken under duress. You must have beaten him to get him to talk."

"Shot him in the toes and ear, actually." I poured myself a cup of coffee.

"No police department, no court, no district attorney would pay any attention to that tape."

"Oh, they'd pay some attention to it. Your father would probably be interested in it, too."

"What's your price?" he said, his voice dripping icicles.

"Not much. I bribe easily. But I want to know the answer to one question before we start talking money. Why? Why would someone like you get involved in something this stupid?"

"Stupid? You think it's stupid?"

"Yes."

"And I suppose you've got another tape machine hidden on you somewhere. If you think I'm going to talk to you, you're crazy."

I put the barrel of the Walther against his cheek and pulled down hard, the front sight cutting through his skin.

"If I convinced Leo to talk, do you really think you're going to be able to hold out on me?"

He started to get up and I pushed him back in his chair.

"Why, Chadway?"

He put a hand to his cheek, saw the blood on his

177

hand and wiped it off on his robe in quick, nervous strokes.

"You're really crazy," he said, his voice cracking like a teenage boy's.

"Maybe, but I'm not recording this, and if you play your cards right, the cops will never hear that tape. Now tell me. Why did you get involved in this whole dumb scheme?"

"It was Dave's fault," he said sullenly.

"Dave Church?"

"Yes, he was always playing the horses, going to the track, betting with that stupid bookie North. He spent hours on his precious racing forms. If he spent as much time studying for exams, he would have been at the top of his class. It was an absolute obsession with him."

"So Church decided to fix the race?"

"No, it was my idea. I told him how easy it would be. It was a game really, that's all it was, a game."

"A game?"

Chadway's voice was picking up speed and emotion. "Yes, I told him I could fix a race and make a lot of money. He wouldn't believe me. It was simple really. We had this great horse at the ranch—"

"Trish's Lamb Chop?"

"Yes. I took him over to Donald Jepson—we'd done business with him for years—and told him what I had planned. At first he wanted no part of it. I told him we'd start doing business with other trainers, and besides, he needed the money badly, so he went along with it, making sure the horse would lose all his early races. Dave and I went to the track, and Jepson pointed out that silly old man that worked for the bookies."

"Johnny Aiello?"

"Yes. Jepson told us how they worked the system, how they drove down the odds if some big bets came in off track. Dave's idea was to wait until they had this big tournament in Reno. That way we could get a really big bet down."

"What about the Alta Group?"

Chadway giggled. I remembered that giggle well. "*Alta*, means *high* in Spanish. We were high on coke when we decided to go through with all this, so I put the horse's ownership under the Alta Group. Our little joke."

"And what about James Widmer? Was he in this too?"

"No, Jimmy would never have had the stomach for anything like this, but when he was injured in the accident, it looked like a perfect opportunity to use his name, so the money wouldn't be traced back to us. Dave introduced me to North as Jimmy, and I placed some bets with him for months before the race, so he wouldn't get suspicious when we made the big one."

"So you made the bet with North, and collected the money from him?"

The giggle came on again. "Yes, I used the same silly wig, glasses, and mustache that Dave did up in Reno. North was such a fool."

"So Dave Church had nothing to do with the murders?"

Chadway waved a palm in the air. "No, as soon as we got the money, he took off for Europe, he was always—"

"Shut up," I said, watching Chadway squirm as I sipped the coffee. "So it all started out as a stupid game."

"Yes, I never meant—"

179

"Shut up," I said again, much louder this time. All a game. I poured more coffee. Chadway perched on the edge of his chair, a student waiting for the bell to ring so he could go out and play with the rest of the kids again.

He cleared his throat. "I don't have a lot of cash myself, but if you'd be willing to—"

"No. The tape is not for sale. To you. You can have that copy, I've got others. You were right about the police. There's not much they could do with the tape; it was all taken illegally. They'd talk to Leo, of course, but some smart lawyer, not Sam Vickers, he's got too much class to handle that kind of garbage, would wiggle you out of most of it. They might tie you into Johnny's death at the track, but even if they did, the most you'd get would be second-degree manslaughter. After all, you weren't trying to kill the old man, just shoot him full of drugs so he'd go to sleep for a while. It was Leo who cracked his neck.

"Don Jepson. Another toughy. There's not any real proof that he was murdered, is there? And Bobby North? From what Leo told me, he handled most of that, after you set up the meeting. Of course there's Connie Jepson, but clever bastard that you are, I'm sure there's nothing to link you to her death. Cops might make a little noise, but they'd be happy to have it closed out as a suicide, just a poor grieving widow who couldn't face life without her husband. So, no matter how deeply involved you are in all of this, it would be tough as hell to pin anything on you, especially if Leo Goens wasn't around.

"That's why I'm not turning the tape over to the cops. I'm giving it to some people in Nevada. Remember I told you they offered a twenty-five thousand dollar reward? They're very serious people. I told Leo all this. I also told him that I was going to see you, tell you the whole story. I told him that you'd either try to buy him off or kill him, that with him dead, you'd be home free. One of you dead would probably satisfy those Nevada folks. Thanks for the coffee, and have a nice day."

25

"You're sure you had absolutely nothing to do with it?" demanded Jane Tobin.

"My hands are clean," I said, "at least figuratively." I went to the sink and rinsed off the flour.

"If I thought you were involved, Nick, I'd go to the police. I really would."

"I wouldn't blame you," I said, putting my hand under her chin and kissing her lightly on the nose. "I did not have anything to do with the death of Keith Chadway."

She searched my eyes for a few seconds, then went back to the paper. The story was somewhere in the back section, appropriately enough near the death notices.

Keith Chadway, twenty-four, son of well-known financier G. K. Chadway, was found in a wooded area of Wunderlich County Park, in the San Mateo Hills. Police estimate he had been dead for at least three days. Young Chadway, a student at Stanford University, had been known to ride his horse in the area. A preliminary report shows that death was caused by a broken neck."

"If it makes you feel any better, Jane, the police did question me. They knew I was down to see him at his house last week." I dropped the floured veal shanks into the hot frying pan.

"What about Leo Goens? Did you tell them about him?"

"Yes, Leo's name came up. He seems to have disappeared. But don't worry. He's too big and too stupid to hide for long. Someone's going to find him."

"You seem awfully calm about all of this, Nick."

"What can I do? I'm not a hypocrite. I'm not sad the bastard is dead, but I didn't kill him. If Leo did, let the cops find him and prove it."

"I still think it was—"

Saved by the bell. I picked up the phone in the hall. "Hello."

"Mr. Polo, this is John Boscacci, calling from Reno."

"Nice to hear from you."

"I received a tape in the mail. It covered that matter we discussed."

"Interesting tape?"

"I thought so. So did several of my associates. We intend to take action on it." He waited, and when I didn't respond, said, "whoever sent the tape didn't identify himself. There's still that twenty-five thousand dollar reward."

"Seems a shame to let it go to waste."

"Any suggestions?"

183

"Well, if whoever did the dirty deed is too bashful to speak up, why don't you give the money to charity?"

"Any favorites?" Boscacci asked.

"There's the Rose Resnick Center for the Blind and Handicapped in San Francisco. They do good work."

"Apparently you do too. Goodbye, Mr. Polo."

By the time I got back to the stove, the frying pan was smoking and the veal shanks were more than just a little overbrowned. I dumped them in the garbage.

"Does that mean we're going out to eat?" Jane said.

"Unless you want to cook."

She stood up and put on her coat. "I was in the mood for French tonight, anyway."

Several obvious responses came to mind, but I just said, "That sounds like a good idea."